SHORT LINE

A novel by
James J. Klekowski

ELLIS AVENUE STUDIOS

Ellis Avenue Studios
2016

Cover design by Todd Engel, Engel Creative
Edited by Käthe Walton
With special thanks to Kevin P. Murphy
and Joann Podkul Murphy

Because of Käthe

SHORT LINE

The bully was dead.

It was a steamy summer morning when they fished his oversized carcass out of the waters of Black Beach, or *Baja Negra*, as the new locals called it. This was an area of the Calumet River so labeled by the neighborhood kids a generation or two before because of the residue left on their naked bodies when they went skinny dipping there rather than make the long trek to Calumet Beach at the bottom end of the Lake Michigan shores on Chicago's southeast side.

The kids had found the mostly submerged corpse bobbing up against an attached ladder of their diving pylon, a huge round concrete cylinder protecting a main support of the Skyway Bridge that passed overhead at this point on the river. Chances are one of the older boys had helped himself to the missing wallet before they alerted the police, but there was no mistaking the identity of the sleeping with the fishes buoy: Joey Miller, left hand man to the 10th Ward alderman and muscle for the last union of any consequence still thriving here.

Everybody knew Joey Miller and anybody who knew him either feared him or hated him or both. He was, as we say, a product of the Chicago Public Schools system. Even worse, he was a life-long product of the southeast side of Chicago, a refuge of the politically and the morally disconnected, the disenfranchised and the discarded souls who were either born here and didn't know better to leave, or were sent here to purgatory and couldn't find their way out. Few people did get out. A few souls stuck around for laughs. Lifers. Like Joey.

Miller got out suddenly, but not the way he would have liked. Who does get to pick and choose their destiny these days? Lieutenant Vic Hanley officially made the I. D., one of more than two dozen of Chicago's finest paying their respects to the beached dead man that early summer morning. A tall, well-built man, not too shabby-looking for being in his mid-sixties. A man among men, with a commanding presence of Irish-Slavic descent, Hanley ran the show and those who knew turned to him for instructions and commands. He had seen enough of this kind of final departure to anticipate more to come in short order. Hanley was also a lifer down here. Out of the late St. Patrick's Parish.

The body was discovered early enough for the local action news teams to flock to the scene, their trucks initially blocking the ambulance assigned to carry the corpse to the coroner's table for further examination. But there was no mistaking the hole on the right side of Miller's bald head, just above and behind his ear, as to cause of death. The vacancy of the man's skull on the opposite side was another clue, even for the rookie cops present. There's no shame in losing your breakfast at the first murder scene after party you may witness. It doesn't get prettier, or easier, as the veterans of the force would have you believe.

The kids must have missed the diamond stud in Joey's remaining lobe when they rifled the body. They also missed the 6 bundles of hundred dollar bills Joey had in his pockets. Guess the boys came from an honest home after all. Looked to be about thirty thousand in cash to Lieutenant Hanley, who ordered the two tech cops wearing plastic gloves to bag the stash as evidence. The police also removed the three handguns from Joey's specially tailored hidden pockets, 2 under his armpits, the other on his right side. The left side trick pocket was empty. Was that the weapon that did this, Hanley wondered to himself? He wouldn't be the only one who also wondered why Joey was wearing a heavy overcoat on such a hot night, in the coming days of the investigation. Rubbing the coat's material between his fingers, Vic recognized the familiar texture of Kevlar.

The morning tugs continued shoving their cargo loads past the scene, causing some waves on the minimal shoreline directly under the bridge superstructure. Cleaning some spittle off of his department-issued safety vest, one of the rookies cracked a joke about the hovering press, some reference to vultures, to break the tension of the moment. Of the people watching at a distance, night workers getting off their shift from the nearby factory, railroad workers from a parked freight train above the viaduct, police, press, the early morning swim team, half of them were on their cell phones or taking pictures of the scene with their cell phones. Do people still buy cameras?

It was getting a little too circus-like. Nobody could do anything about the helicopters, but at least they couldn't get under the bridge. Their noise and the echoes were overpowering, though. Hanley ordered the location cleared. He'd had enough and WOULD SOMEBODY GET THOSE DAMNED CHOPPERS OUT OF HERE?? Like screaming at windmills. Besides, somebody had to wake the alderman, and all that background noise would not do.

Alderman Antonio J. Coronado was already awake. His wife, Lydia, had heard the first reports of the discovered corpse from the kitchen TV set while preparing breakfast for her husband of nineteen years. By the time she reached the bedroom doorway on the second floor of their modest brick home in Hegewisch, Lydia saw that her husband was seated on the side of the bed, on his cell phone, nodding. Tony gave her a look to let her know that he disapproved of her interrupting his call.

"They found a dead body in the Calumet under the Skyway," she announced, and returned to her duties downstairs. She would let the children sleep a while longer. It was a hotter than usual Wednesday summer morning in Chicago and day camp at church was on their kids' schedule for the bulk of the day. But in this household Wednesday meant only one thing, City Council day.

Antonio's phone conversation was interrupted by an incoming call, anyway, which he had to take. It had a 744 prefix. City business.

"What's up, Lieutenant?" Pause. The news sank in. The still young-looking, firm but on the short side politician got up and parted the dark curtains, peering out the window facing the street, adjusting his eyes to the bright morning light. He spotted the squad car parked in front of his awaiting black limo.

7

"I appreciate that, Vic. I really do." Antonio instinctively adjusted his nuts. "You coming down to the Hall?" He walked over to the bathroom door. "Yeah, it's the big one. I'll see you then." He left the phone on the dresser beside the door and entered the tiled room, flicking on the light switch. About to close the door, he thought better of it, and brought the phone in with him.

I'm still not sure why, but I got Hanley's next call. Maybe he thought he owed me something for saving his life, a couple of years back when we were caught in a shootout with the last of the old Latin Counts, in South Chicago. Maybe he just wanted to know my whereabouts at the time of Joey's passing. I don't ask cops questions and they don't tell me things I don't want to hear. Usually. Sometimes.

"Did you catch the news about our Joey?" Vic tried to be cute. "We just fished him out of the river under the Skyway. I thought you might like to know that." Real cute.

"I'm watching on 'GN. You look fat on TV."

"The choppers piss me off."

"Takes you back to 'Nam, huh?" I could be cute, too. Hanley had a couple of college deferments back in the day, like any number of our recent national office-holding politicos. The sounds of buzzing drones under the bridge made me hold the phone away from my head.

"How did he get it?" I wanted to get to the point.

"One large in the head."

"Front?" Pause.

"Right side."

"He knew the guy."

"Yeah, our Joey didn't let just anybody get that close."

"Burn marks?"

"Not that I saw, but some of that washes off in the water."

"Did he get it on the beach or over the side of the 100th Street Bridge and float down?" Hanley signaled to a pair of officers to check out the vehicular bascule bridge to the south.

"The coroner's office will tell. Got time for breakfast?"

"I'll meet you at Sonny's in an hour."

"Make it half, I gotta get down to the Hall."

"I might be a little late. I've got to stop at Calumet Bakery for some doughnuts." Hanley thought I made a crack and laughed. I hung up my flip phone and turned to look at the indentation in the pillow beside me. She left for work early again. Well, it was the big day. Why did I let her use those old lace pillowcases? Too scratchy. I made time for a shower, but didn't bother with the stubble.

Catching my reflection in the full-length mirror in the upstairs hallway between our bedroom and the bath, I took a brief inventory of the body impolitic from top to bottom. Hair a little long but no real grays, just that dark blond or light brown shade pre-mop top, easier to brush than to comb. Good face, kind of chiseled but fairly clean-shaven now, just a hint of a dimple in the chin. Good physique, narrow waist but not too hour-glassy, flat stomach a thirty year old would kill for, more of a shower than a grower in the cock department and a tight end that looked great in jeans. Athletic legs but not bulky, toes not too hairy, clean-cut toenails, not bad for a thirty-nine year old of the hetero persuasion. Any questions?

Up front, let me say that I know the difference between a homicide and a murder, the former having no suspect. Murder, the word, has more impact. That use of words may have a difference to the law enforcement professionals, but any family losing a member to a crime could care less.

Joey Miller had been voted 'most likely to succeed' by his graduating class at James H. Bowen High School in 1995. Considering that the school had mostly Black and Latino students, it always tweaked my interest that one of the very few white guys would gain such popularity. What votes he couldn't buy or steal were wrenched out of his classmates under threat of reprisals from Joey's interracial gang of misfits. By that time there were few students and teachers alike who didn't know that Joey got what he wanted because of the legend he had built up around himself since his early grade school days, much of it just a legend, but with enough real intimidation that was paid off with broken windows, broken bones, slashed tires, torched garages and more unsavory escapades buried in his permanent record.

The Bowen High School revolving-door administrators, while keeping an eye on the up and coming lad, took a hands off approach to his discipline as he was, and remains, the greatest all-around football player in the school's history. Jocks ruled then as they still do now in schools across this great city. They get the pep rallies that are mandatory attendance for all students and the awards shows, both conveniently set during school hours; they get the smoking fundraisers and even priority funds from downtown. They want it, they get it. Got it?

Miller wasn't even Joey's actual name. I had to look it up once a couple of years back in an obscure family history for background on a story. It was some lengthy Bohemian-sounding moniker which I've since forgotten how to spell, but it was shortened to Miller by the gatekeepers at Ellis Island nearer the turn of the last century. It didn't matter. The boy bully who became a man bully was all Chicago. He didn't have a clue as to his own roots or care for that matter to look back, except over his shoulder. Joey always had appeared to be emotionally detached from his family at an early age. They were decent people, humble and God-fearing, and provided a nice enough place in Calumet Heights for him to crash for most of his youth, but useless to an angry kid on the way up. Where he got that anger streak from I never could find out. The streets called and he made himself the answer.

Joey didn't have to worry about failure on the playing field because of the iron fist he ruled with behind his coaches' backs through the years. It seemed like it, anyway. In their freshman year a fellow player blew a crucial pass just before half time during a home game with Bowen's chief rival in their division. In the second half, the rival team failed to score once, didn't even get over the 50-yard line again, and Bowen went on to victory. For the rest of the season. For the rest of Miller's three years at Bowen. Rumor had it, and rarely fails, that Joey and two of his boys had a private chat with butterfingers in the locker room during half time. While the two goons held their fellow teammate, Miller shoved his hand down the kid's pants and into his jockstrap gripping the boy's balls with that iron fist Joey was known for, promising that, if he blew another pass, "Dees are goin' home wit' me."

––––––––––––––––––––

Before hopping onto the Skyway for the ride downtown, Alderman Coronado checked in at his offices on Commercial Avenue. Once a dilapidated retail outlet, the Fink building survived the Great Depression, a couple of fires and more recently, the Great Recession, when all of its tenants lost their leases to make way for a phone store, a bank chain boutique outlet and, on the second floor, the domain of the newly installed alderman of the 10th Ward.

As the first Latino alderman of the heavily Latino 10th Ward, Coronado had been a perennial candidate for more than a decade. He only became alderman two years before by the luck of being the loudest voice at hand when the previous alderman died of a massive heart attack while in office. Funny thing about that, the previous alderman was never sick a day in his life. You just never know.

The mayor, from whom all blessings flow, while trying to shore up Latino support for his own upcoming reelection, reached across the aisle, as they say, to handpick Coronado for the job. Up until that moment Antonio had been the most outspoken non-office holder against the current administration, and wouldn't have had his calls returned from the mayor on a prayer. Things change.

Exiting his limo, which had pulled in and parked just ahead of a people mover, one of those new, black Sprinters, and a delivery truck, Coronado quickly stepped through the awaiting press gauntlet without comment. The alderman passed by a uniformed officer at the doorway to his offices. He climbed the stairs to the main hallway, where as usual, a small, local crowd had gathered for the chance to meet with the alderman to request favors. This abnormal hero worship is not unique to the 10th Ward. Every alderman in each of the city's 50 wards holds court on an almost daily basis, approving and denying favors to the masses, their tax-paying constituents. Everybody stands when the alderman passes by, the reverence may pay off later. Most in line had seen the early morning news, by this time including a mini-history of the neighborhood and Coronado's sudden rise to political stardom.

Several of Coronado's precinct captains who had also caught the morning news gathered at the doorway to the inner sanctum, in earnest hopes of succeeding the late Joey M. This mob included the two goons from Joey's high school days, Bernard P and Eduardo Z, but I preferred calling them Twiddle Don't and Twiddle Do. Not to their faces, of course. They, and a few other goons, had all stayed close across the years.

Deliveries of floral wreaths and tributes to Joey's untimely passing were already lining the hallway, with more arriving by the minute. A parting of the guard was made as Antonio approached. The blond goon, Bernard P grabbed the doorknob and opened the wood framed, privacy glass-paned door for the alderman to pass through. As he entered the reception area outside his office, it was business as usual. A couple of secretaries to his right were preparing the day's workload for the hallway crowd. Erlinda Sanchez, Antonio's private secretary, and sister-in-law, was exiting his office in the rear as he came upon the doorway. Though smartly dressed for an office job, Lynn was more like executive material in style and poise, and almost a head taller than her brother-in-law. She never did lose those fine looks of hers. Everybody had called her 'Lynn' since grade school.

"Your council case is already on your desk." Erlinda stood at a desk just outside Antonio's doorway, rearranging papers. She gave a look to the other secretaries' hushed whispers at the far end of the room, and then entered her own office to the left of the alderman's.

"Has my mother been in yet?" he called out as he sat down at his desk in the center of the large, spacious room, a window flanking either side of the centerpiece. Antonio pulled out a set of keys and opened a locked bottom drawer of the desk, revealing a clipboard with papers attached.

"She's downstairs at the bank. I'm surprised you two didn't pass each other." Erlinda came back into Tony's office. "The press wants a statement."

"Didn't they get enough of me at the governor's gig last week?" She waited for a useful reply. "I'll make a statement downtown after the City Council meeting. Have our guys move the flowers into the meeting room. And close the drapes. I don't want to look at 'em. C'mon, *hermana*." He got up with clipboard in hand and stepped back into the main inner office and, to the left of both their office doorways, entered what looked like a supply room. Erlinda followed.

"What's up?" she asked as Coronado checked his wristwatch, pulling back a set of floor-length velour curtains on the far wall to reveal a walk-in safe, built by lawyers back in the '30's when they were more trusted than banks with customers' valuables. He whipped through the combination and unlocked the double doors. Erlinda had already quietly closed the office door.

"Joey had money on him. I want to know how much." Along with sensitive papers and files on shelves and other odds and ends from previous tenants, the safe also contained neat stacks of bundled cash. Campaign contributions and tributes, amassed over the years, campaign to campaign, the necessary grease for a well-run machine, even though just a small one.

Tony checked the piles of cash against the ledger on the clipboard, running his fingers down the columns of stacked money. "Here." He paused over one short stack. "No, that was the benefit in June." Coronado continued to the next short stack. "One, two, three, four, five, six, seven, eight. Forty thousand. Hanley guessed thirty." Exchanging a look, they both considered the results of their money inventory. Exiting the safe, Antonio closed the doors tightly. As they stepped into the outer room, Maria Sosa, a pretty young secretary who was new to the ward office, greeted them.

"Alderman, your mother called to tell you she's in the car."

Coronado handed off the clipboard to Erlinda. "Thank you, Maria." Antonio stepped back into his office to snatch his briefcase.

Maria just stood there. "Was there anything else, Maria?" Lynn asked.

"Is he really dead? Mr. Miller, I mean?"

"Yes, dear. I believe so."

"Good."

Sonny's Inn was a neighborhood institution since the 1950's when the old Illinois Central railroad station was converted to its present day purpose as a killer hamburger joint. It was also THE watering hole for three generations of local politicos and wannabees. The walls were adorned with trophies, political mementos, faded photos and headlines from something called newspapers, hailing the local winners and losers alike. In a few of the black and white photos and fading newspapers, the deer-in-the-headlights guy looks like a younger version of your narrator, before middle age had started to set in. The bar had seen better days, but so had most of its patrons.

I arrived first and, finding the main entrance still locked, checked my watch. Yes, I still wear one. The place didn't technically open for another 2 hours, so I walked around to the side entrance, through the kitchen. Sam Osorio, the proprietor, was taking stock of buns in his storeroom.

"Hey! Big news today, huh? I'm gonna open early for the press crowd, you think? I texted the invites myself!"

"Get any replies, Sam?"

"ABC. NBC. 'GN. They got the dough."

"Too bad you don't have a helipad out back." The door behind me opened. It was Hanley.

"You got company," Sam said as he returned to his inventory duties. He didn't like cops any more than anybody else who didn't know any better.

"When you getting a replacement for that expired state sticker on your personal vehicle, Osorio?" the lieutenant said as he passed through the kitchen on a beeline to the dining room. I hated it when Hanley played bad cop. I could hear the little man mutter something humble sounding under his breath as I followed. Hanley chose the booth farthest from the kitchen. You'd think he wanted some privacy but I figured he just wanted to make Sam walk the length of the place to serve us.

"So who got the assignment?" I thought I'd open the conversation. Hanley pulled out the props he never went anywhere without: his pack of Camels, that old flip lighter of his with an etched U. S. S. Essex on the front, and the stand-by glass ashtray with a Phil

Schmidt's logo embossed in the center. Phil Schmidt's was another landmark eatery just across the state line in Hammond that went belly up just before the casino moved in. Vic gave me a withered glance.

"You mean who avoided it." He lit up as Sam delivered a pair of cups of coffee. Yeah, it's still against the law in this town to light up inside a restaurant. The innkeeper was used to us.

"What you boys want to eat?" he asked in that slightly old world accent of his. I wasn't sure if it was Spanish or Italian or what, it just sounded like it fit the joint.

"Scrambled eggs, toasted English muffin, bacon crispy." Hanley graciously blew his smoke away from us.

"I'll have the same, Sam, and hash browns, please." Hanley glanced my way and gave me a smirk at my manners. Sam returned to the kitchen. I returned a smile. "What do you mean, 'avoided'?" We were alone in the room, but Hanley shifted himself closer to me.

"You think any career dick wants this disaster on his sheet? They gave it to Sasuta and his rookie partner, a, what's-his-name, the tall Hispanic," he said disdainfully. "Old Sasuta's the closest detective to retirement in the district. This won't affect his pension and who's gonna care about his partner?"

"You think they're already preparing for a cover-up?" Vic held up both hands as a stop sign.

"I think the waiting line to end Joey is too long to figure for the brass. They want this 'investigation' done before he's down six feet."

"Miller picked a great time to get killed," I said flatly.

"Killed! That was a hit and about fucking time that filth got stepped on, anyway." Hanley leaned back, tapping his cigarette butt into his ashtray. "Ah, did you do the deed, Dano?" Hanley got a kick out of calling me 'Dano' as if I were a sidekick character from Hawaii 5-0.

I gave the lieutenant a long look. "I was gonna ask you the same thing, Vic," I said with a little laugh. "How long have you known me?"

"Everybody has a breaking point, kid. You two go way back, from what you've let me in on. You wouldn't be at the top of anybody's list, anyhow. I had to ask. Just so I know, where were you last night? You don't have to answer that without a lawyer present." He smiled. I was being played.

"I was at Polish Jay's." I smiled back.

"That's about three blocks from where Joey's body was found."

"Yeah, more like five blocks and on the wrong side of the river. I know gunshots when I hear them, but I wouldn't have heard a thing over the trains."

He was enjoying this too much. That was the first time I noticed the slight tremor in Vic's hands, as he returned his coffee cup to its saucer. I remembered that same involuntary motion in my mom's hands a decade or so back. I suddenly felt a lot closer to Hanley than I had before, with all time had already piled on us.

Sam came back with our food and, wiping his hands on his white apron as he went, unlocked the front door, just in time for a few newsy types to enter with their equipment in tow and ooh and aah over the interior political decorations from before their time. Slumming tourists with press credentials.

"Don't get me wrong, but I had to ask. I know you know how to use a weapon, Dano."

"No offense taken, Lieutenant."

"Whoever did Joey made his bones last night."

"Or this morning." Again with that withered look of his, like the world and I were so naive. When will I shut up?

We finished our meal before Hanley's driver came in to remind him of the time. "Gotta go," Vic said as he rose from the table.

"Catch you later, Lieu."

"That's my line. You sure Polish Jay will back up your alibi?" Grabbing up his props he smiled and exited the restaurant.

I got stuck with the bill.

Politics has been a full-time spectator sport in Chicago since the first outsiders took over power from the locals by voting them out back in 1833 in a tavern at Wolf Point. A hundred years ago each ward had two aldermen to gather the clout, spread the wealth to their cronies, supporters, masters and sycophants. Everybody got theirs, except for the actual taxpayers who paid for it all, twice. I may sound jaded but the facts are there to read for anybody bothering to crack open a history book. We proudly repeat our mistakes every chance we get at every election cycle. We deserve the corrupted wretches we're stuck with in office, because we hired them! 'The gem of the prairie' was a name given this town a long time ago. It was as much of an oxymoron then as it is today. Don't mind me, I'm just on a rant. If I ever got out of here myself I'd probably shrivel up and die for want of the corruption. I live for this stuff like any real Chicagoan!

I paid Sam and left a healthy tip on the table, nodding to the pressies crowding two tables near the doorway. One of the newsies gave me a look as I passed and pointed quizzically to a faded newspaper hanging over the bar, but I paid him no heed. Looked like one of the sons of a local anchor on Channel 11, Chicago's PBS outlet. I had to wonder what was up with that new-grown beard the kid reporter was touting?

Starting up my car I drove west a couple of blocks to Commercial Avenue, the faded business district of South Chicago. Taking a right turn at the light I found a spot a few blocks ahead and pulled in just in front of the office, under the shadow of the Immaculate Conception bell tower. I left the windows rolled down to keep the car cool as the morning started to warm up.

Before the mall infestation struck the Chicago area after World War II, nearly a dozen mini-downtowns were the commercial hubs of neighborhoods across the city. South Chicago, specifically Commercial Avenue, was a grand example. In its heyday between the world wars, South Chicago boasted nine theaters, a half-dozen department stores, men's and women's clothing shops, restaurants, a number of banks and building & loans, butcher shops and bakeries, all serving a growing community of ethnic diversity, even if all the ethnics didn't actually get along. Dozens of churches, schools, fraternal organizations and social services rounded out the lives of the mostly blue collar, mostly steel mill or shipping or rail workers who called this home for themselves and their Americanized families.

A sign on the window beside the door I entered read: 'Home of The Calumet News Service'. The writers, reporters and photographers who worked here just called it 'The Service', though some of the older guys knew it as 'The Calumet'.

"Mr. Larry's already asking for your copy, Nick!" greeted Louise, our secretary/office manager/sounding board/confidant. In her late sixties and with no desire of retiring, Louise Beavers was a grandmother several times over and took care of this office with the same gentle but firm love that made her blessed in the eyes of her family and church community.

"What's the rush? This story just started cooking!" I scanned the three TV sets attached to the far wall, no sound, to see what was being covered locally.

"You know how he gets when the downtown crews come here snooping for headlines." Louise handed me a small pile of messages, smiling. I noticed the top message from the Chicago Daily News, again. She gave me a shrewd look.

"How do you think this got on top?" I inquired, already knowing the answer.

"How do you expect to get ahead turning your nose up at jobs from downtown?" Louise replied. We had been through this before, a couple of times.

"I'm not as ambitious as you think, Louise. I like it here!" I stepped over to my desk and slipped the messages onto a spindle with the other myriad messages I was behind on answering and pulled out a laptop from a bottom drawer, flipping the device open.

"You're just comfortable here is all, Nick. Too comfortable if you're askin' me. You gotta go see what's out there and take that chance!" Her phone rang. "Calumet News Service. How may I direct your call?"

I got to work on my copy. Along with a weekly newspaper release, the Calumet produced a daily news blog for and about the neighborhood, which stretched from South Shore, roughly 79th Street south to the Chicago border at 135th Street. Local news, local color, with an occasional hot story covered by the downtown bureaus and once in a great while, picked up nationally. Not so often for the latter since the mills closed. Today would be a biggie news day, and some national outlet would pick up our blog, but my mind drifted back on its own steam to a time before. I kept trying to focus on the work in front of me.

Joey Miller's future was made during a small stint he did at Cook County Jail shortly after 'graduating' high school. A suburban outfit man was detained at the jail on some outstanding warrant, and without the mob muscle he was used to for personal protection, wouldn't have made it through the first night without Joey watching his back. Maybe they were both just at the right place at the right time. Who can say? The mob guy, maybe the mob for that matter, didn't forget Joey Miller. Someone even got his charges scrapped. Joey got a collections job from his new friends in the suburban syndicate, kind of a probationary position. It wasn't long after that a local union in need of muscle became Joey's new playground. Who says doing time at Cook County doesn't look good on your résumé?

———

The black limo picked up speed after passing through the northbound tollbooth on the Skyway. A police cruiser led the way. The Alderman of the 10th Ward of the City of Chicago was on his way to the weekly meeting of the City Council, where another 49 aldermen more or less divvied out the favors garnered and paid forward from the last weekly meeting. Not in the light of day, please! After all, these public servants didn't get to their positions by hook or by crook alone. Subtlety, by all means necessary.

This august chamber had, in its storied past, held witness to open and blatant racism, theft, graft on an epic scale, rubber stampism, shouting members standing on their desks, and occasionally some actual city business for the good of the public, somewhere among its vast accomplishments. Once upon a time, a powerful mayor had the place bugged, but by now you all know what to expect from rumors in the press.

It was just after rush hour and the ride downtown wouldn't take too long. Coronado was leafing through the multiple items to be brought up and voted on at the meeting, including one ballsy whopper he had drafted, co-sponsored and planned to present to the full council, skipping the proper committee layers. The window between the driver and the back seat rose to a closed position. The alderman's mother was pressing the button.

A bespectacled woman in her late 70's or older perhaps, Angela Maria Serros-Coronado was smaller in frame than her persona would let on. Not a hair out of place, not a trace of grey. The backbone of her *familia*, she remained the force behind the man. First her husband, and when he wore out, her son. At all times a serious woman in a serious world.

"'Tonyo. I want to talk about this Joey Miller business before you get to your meeting in City Hall." 'Tonyo had been her pet name for her only child since he was a small *nino*.

Coronado didn't look away from his papers. "They told me he's dead, Ma. That's all I know about it. Let his family make the final arrangements."

"I know you're going to need another Joey if you want to win an election this time." That got his attention. "Not everybody is going to die to get out of your way up the ladder, *mijo*." He turned to his Mother seated next to him in the well-appointed limo, the papers in his lap.

"Mama, Joey was your idea from the start. Seven years ago when he dropped in from nowhere I didn't ask for him and I didn't like the move. My supporters didn't like it, even the ones who stayed on with us afterwards. Downtown didn't like it, but there was Miller in our camp and now he isn't. You know he's going to be even more trouble for us dead than he was alive, Mama?"

"'Tonyo, you know he opened doors for you when nobody was talking to us, not even our own. He did what had to be done."

"At what cost, Ma? Then let it be done and we'll give him a big funeral send-off, for all of it, just like they did for Colosimo and Torrio and the other great thugs this city produced. He'll get all that and more. The flowers are already piling up at our doorstep."

"The dead don't need gratitude, *mijo*, not from the living. They need peace. They need honor."

After a pause. "Why should the dead get what the living can't have, Mama?"

"What?" She was firm.

"Letting him be that close to us for all that time made everything we did dirty, Mama. He made all of us and everything we stand for unclean." Coronado was on the brink of losing it. Gesturing with his hands, "He made me dirty. Me!" He returned to his papers.

"*Mijo*, everything is going to be alright now." Her voice built up. "You had to go through hell to get to this point, to get to where you must be now. Every great man does. We all did with you. It's only a short walk now to victory. To everything we - you've worked for, it all must go on. You were chosen. Even your mayor saw that. Nothing can stop you, 'Tonyo." He can't believe a word but he has to swallow it, just the same. There's no time for argument. There's nothing to argue. He was the chosen one. Coronado steels himself for the next gauntlet. Mother and son exchanged an understanding look. *"Mi Corazon, mijo, para ti. Todo."*

The limo pulled to a stop near the LaSalle Street entrance to City Hall. A murder of press (which also works for crows) had converged on the curb beside the limo. On a double-knock from inside, the driver opened the rear passenger side door.

The Alderman of the 10th Ward of the City of Chicago briskly exited the limo followed closely by the media, nodding to their overlapping questions, camera lights and flashes seeming to lead him into the building. The driver returned to his seat behind the wheel. *"Norte. Vamos,"* ordered the single passenger in the rear seat as the limo reentered traffic, heading northbound on LaSalle Street.

———

Since it was still technically Wednesday morning, and I already picked up the doughnuts, I thought I'd head over to the Calumet Park field house early for the weekly meeting of the Southeast Chicago Historical Society irregulars, a group of mostly retired locals who got together to update their memories, reminisce about the good old days, or just gossip about the comings and goings of the neighborhood they'd called home for most if not all of their lives. They also cleaned the place once a week, the day before regular Thursday visiting hours for the public.

I filed my reactionary, vitriol-filled, brutally honest obit-story on the late Joey Miller with Louise who electronically sent it upstairs to Larry Galica's office. Our crusty editor had worked decades before on the Daily Calumet newspaper here in South Chicago, at the time the nation's oldest community newspaper, when the vast steel industry employed 30,000 men and women and the skies lit up at night with blast furnaces and slag. All before my time.

In my rush out the door I hadn't noticed the breaking news reports on the still-silent TV monitors as I exited the office. Each was broadcasting split screens, Coronado arriving at City Hall and a more local breaking story just on the other side of the river.

As I drove onto the superstructure of the 95th Street bridge, I passed my favorite forbidden pleasure, Calumet Fisheries. When I get the chance remind me to tell you about their smoked shrimp. I kid you not, it's the crack of shellfish!

My car tires made that unmistakable sound of rubber on roadbed suddenly gliding across metal gratings echoing off the waters below. Hot mornings like this made the waters shine like diamonds. At the crown of the bridge I saw a crowd gathered down ahead, off to the right, just past the tracks. Squads, an ambulance and a media tower or two were parked in the alleyway just east of the lead switches to the Short Line Railroad yard. I drove by the mob the cops were holding back and pulled into the next available parking space.

As I walked around the throng of gawkers and press as if I owned the place, a younger Black cop moved from his position to stop my advance.

"Hey buddy! This isn't open to the public!"

"I appreciate that, Officer…" I scanned his nametag quickly. "Bland."

"That's 'Brand' sir." Me, without my reading glasses. A sergeant farther ahead in the lot called out.

"HAROLD!" The officer turned towards his superior. "It's okay. He owns the place!" I was in the lot before the press could make their move, but I could hear them mispronouncing my name. I hoped they weren't live on air but I didn't turn back to find out.

"Hey Bill, what's the – " I caught it out of the corner of my eye. A stretcher emerging from the doorway, being carried out of the second floor apartment. Not an easy maneuver on wooden stairs that take a sharp right halfway down. There was an officer and a paramedic at either end struggling to keep the whole thing from coming down by itself. Ahead of them, already at the bottom of the stairs, was an officer hustling a short Black dude with a long lens camera strung around his neck, off the premises. My camera boy from a past life!

"It's not good, Nick." Bill didn't let go of my hand. He firmly put his frame between me and the scene of something. "I heard the address call on my car radio and came over. I thought it might be you, ya know, but it's some guy I guess you rented the place to." I knew he was talking to me but I didn't hear a thing. I must have had the dumbest look on my face, like somebody just pulled down my pants on the playground at recess. My eyes and the cameraman's crossed paths as he was escorted back to the sidewalk.

I heard my voice ask "Overdose?"

"Looked strangled to me, Nicky. Hey, Nick!"

I finally turned and looked at his face. Bill Jankowski. Billy. Mid-forties now, already a little grey in that military cropped reddish blond hair of his. Still in shape and a sergeant to boot. Those years working for old man Buchanan had paid off. We knew each other after the Vrdolyak dynasty came to its end of keeping the 10th Ward alderman's seat warm, and the old political warhorse from out of the past, John J. Buchanan, had won the office back in a runoff. If the old man didn't care for you he could be a son of a bitch, make life difficult in and out of the ward. If he liked you, you and everything you touched were golden. For some reason I was platinum in those halcyon days gone by. Maybe not so much now.

"Nicky. Where you been? Nobody call you?"

"Breakfast with Vic Hanley at Sonny's. He let me know about… that one." I nodded towards the Skyway Bridge, to our south, indicating the site of Joey's floating remains earlier that morning. "Did you say strangled, Bill?"

Bill nodded. "Knotted rope is what I seen."

I winced. "Who the hell would want to kill Leon? What the fuck is in the water this morning?" I got a little loud.

"Don't look like no robbery. Not much in there. His younger brother found him. Called it in. We already checked him out."

"Leon was the oldest. Their ma threw him out again, a couple a months ago. He couldn't get anything out of her trailer except what he walked out with. I wasn't doing anything with the place since the Colonel, so... So why the press, and that little camera bug?"

"Like they give a shit about this 'hood outside a election time, right? They were here anyway, I guess. Joey goin' down was big news for 'em."

I liked the sound of 'Joey was' and my slight smirk gave it away. "Yeah, was."

"So, where were you last night again, Nicky?" I smiled a bigger smirk to myself.

With a resigned sigh, I said, "I was playing with trains, Sergeant Jankowski." I patted his shoulder stripes with some pride and a small smile. "Be good." Giving him a familiar nod I stepped over to Leon's younger brother, Ernesto, who was standing alone beside the ambulance as the stretcher reached the opened back doors.

Coming from behind him I put my right hand on his left shoulder. "Hey. I'm sorry, 'Nesto." He gave me a look somewhere between anguish and rage and we watched as the paramedics loaded his brother's bagged body into the ambulance.

"You know I was stayin' wit'im?"

"Yeah. He asked me. I said 'Okay'."

"I crashed wit' a frien' las' night, you know? I shudda be'n here."

Maybe not, 'Nesto. Maybe not." We stepped out of the way as the ambulance prepared to pull out.

"You go way back wid'im, right?"

"Yeah, ten years or so. When he was outta the Counts already." The crowd was clearing out. We started walking towards the street. A few press were still lingering but I couldn't see camera boy for the forest. "The press want to talk to you, 'Nesto. Do you want to talk to them?" Ernesto shook his head.

"I gotta call Ma. I wanna be the one ta tell 'er." I caught the eye of Sergeant Jankowski and shook my head, indicating the press. He got it and started to break the remainder up. I steered 'Nesto's short-built frame towards the low stone abutment running alongside the property and we worked our way over and onto the grass. Walking around the long, one-story wood-frame building that once was a dock-working drinking man's bar fronting 95th Street, we moved towards the back, near the bottom of the steps to the former stable some previous owner had converted to apartments for the transient train men from the steam era.

"Need anything outta there?" I motioned to the second floor.

Ernesto shook his head. "You knew about the bi thing wit' Leon, right?' he asked a bit defensively.

"Yeah. That was never an issue with me, man. You need a ride? Some dough?"

"Nah, I got mine over dare on N." He pointed to a beater on the street just east of us. It looked older than he was. I pulled out my wallet anyway. These 30-something guys worked 6-day weeks and were still always hard up for cash.

"Here. Here's a hundred, for gas, you'll need it. Take my card, too."

"T'anks, man." Shoving the stash in the front pocket of his worn jeans, Ernesto gave me a quick, hard hug, the kind sports figures give each other, with one arm each reaching over to pat the others' back, the second pair of arms between them, just to be sure their junk would never accidentally touch.

"Let me know what plans your family makes, okay? I'll be there."

"Yup." I could see he was holding it in and couldn't break down in front of another guy. His eyes were ready to go. He turned and started for his car.

"Don't forget to call me."

"Yeah, man." This last line was given over his shoulder as 'Nesto walked across the empty lots between the bar and Avenue N, head down, picking up speed in his steps. Some guys have to be like that to survive down here, I guess, embarrassed at being human. I looked back at the two flat, the yellow police tape flapping in the breeze. The door was ajar; the techs still inside working. I could see the flash of the evidence camera go off.

Stepping towards the stairs, I thought better of it and instead made my way back to the car, walking close to the eastern exterior of the old bar, between it and a one-story house, out of sight of the crowd. The narrow passage between the one-story buildings came in handy for a quick get-away, I thought. I pulled out my flip phone and almost walked directly into camera boy's rogue long lens.

"Smile, Daniels!" Yeah, it was B. J. King, lead stalker for the Daily News, looking way too young for as old as I knew he was. "Ah... You know I'm kiddin' ya, man!" I knew enough about cameras to know I was too close for that length of lens to get off a shot, anyway. I sidestepped him and crossed the sidewalk and the front of my car before he could try anything. "Don' be like that, man! Aw, c'mon!"

I had left the car unlocked and hopped in, shutting the door and starting the motor. Ever drive an '88 Lincoln Continental? Like driving the smoothest 4-wheel yacht you have ever imagined. I shifted the car into drive, my foot still on the break pedal, when there was a knock on the passenger side window. Pressing the window controls with my left hand, I rolled it halfway down. "What?" I inquired.

"You know me, Daniels! C'mon, man. Open up! Shit! Don't you be leavin' me hangin'!" I snapped the locks into the 'up' position, as they had automatically shut when the car was shifted into drive, which it still was in. He popped the door open and bounced on the passenger seat, all smiles. "How you been, man? Long time no see!"

"How do you still do this for a living, King? Where's all that self-respect I keep hearing your people singing about out there?" That should set him off.

"Why you ungrateful white man!" he laughed. "After all I did for you back in the day-ee!"

"What are you, fifty-five now?"

"Slow down, five-oh! I'll be fifty in November and I'm looking forward to a nod from you in that rag you write for."

"You should live so long." I had things to do and this was not getting them done. "Didn't the News learn anything from the Sun-Times and fire all you camera bugs a long time ago?"

"You gotta see what I got this morning, man. Stop the presses. This is it!" He held the back of his camera up for me to see the oversized video screen, the long lens propped up against his right thigh. He started exposing his captures, what some people 'back in the day' might call pictures, one by one. An overall view of the scene under the Skyway. The pylon in the foreground, tugs across the river in the background. A little closer. Now even closer, past the police line. Like any artist, Brent's images told the entire story without a word uttered. The long lens shots kicking in. The drag marks from the water. Close-ups of the head and the vacant cavity on one side. Close-ups of the half-naked kids draped in their towels. "I can sell that one to the north side crowd, man!" Two officers checking out the kids and their belongings. A hand over his lens, had to be an officer's. "Damn cop!" A wide shot of the apartment, Leon's naked body beside the couch. A close-up of the thick, old knotted rope and welts on his neck. "The nationals will want this stuff, boy!" Suddenly the images went red.

I lifted my foot off the break and stepped on the gas pedal, gliding out of the parking lane. The automatic locks kicked in again from the motion.

"Hey man! My ride's back there!"

I gave it a moment. "Erase the apartment shots, King." I increased our speed, heading due east towards the intersection of Ewing and 95th. Our light changed to yellow. I swerved around an affiliate news camera truck.

"Whatchu doin' man! You crazy or sumptin'?

"Do it, Brent!" When exactly does an immensely talented photographer choose to sell his soul to become a photojournalist? Was he wearing that Pulitzer under his shirt? Do they give out actual medals or is it a scroll or something?

"I ain't doin' shit, you crazy – STOP!" The light changed to red. I floored the Lincoln. While the most recent models available have greater selection in appointments, technology and aerodynamics, there just isn't anything on the road these days that can top the eight cylinders under this hood and the sheer size of its all-metal frame for serious intimidation in traffic. Why, pedestrians across the nation have been known to stop what they're doing, point and watch as the LC rolls by. It's in a class all by itself. And I don't want a discussion about the Crown Victoria.

I pressed the palm of my hand on the horn embedded in the steering wheel and held it down. We sailed across the intersection, avoiding the cross traffic screeching to a stop.

"Let me the fuck outta here! I'm not playin' wit' you now! This is lawyer shit!"

"All of it, Jonesee!" To make my point I turned my head and smiled at Brent as the car sailed across the railroad tracks banking to the right, headed into Calumet Park. I was going that way, anyway. I could make out beads of sweat breaking out across his forehead.

"FUCK YOU MAN! THIS IS MY WORK! I MADE YOU, MAN. YOU FORGET THAT?" I looked back at where we were going, making the sharp left bank onto the eastbound roadway at the split, the right front wheel just dusting up against the curb.

"WE'RE RUNNING OUT OF ROAD, BRENT!" I had to speak up as I had rolled all the windows down. Original motors on those babies.

"IT'S YOUR CAR, MAN! THIS IS CRAZY!" King was cradling his very expensive camera close to his chest. The lake was in view now, shimmering ahead. "THIS IS A FUCKIN' CLASSIC, DANNY! DON'T!"

"TEN SECONDS!" A hundred years ago, we'd already be in Lake Michigan at this point on the road. Calumet Park was the private estate of the Taylor Family, Douglas Taylor being an early developer and promoter of the area. The current field house was built on the spot where their mansion once stood. Quite a lovely house, from the historic photographs I've seen. Nice, big veranda. In fact, after a rainstorm, the lake often covered parts of Ewing Avenue, before the landfills made what is today the ninth largest park in the Chicago Park District system.

King kept chanting 'NO! NO! NO!' as if that was going to stop my sweet behemoth midnight blue Lincoln. As the main drive took a soft right I made the slight left across the oncoming lane into the long load parking lot when I pressed on the brakes. Not a squeal out of them. My mechanic had that touch you don't find everywhere. A real artist at his craft.

"OH HELL!" I heard myself scream as I realized I had forgotten about the blind spot just at the top of the ramp! I didn't know if there was an open ramp at the waterline or not! I resigned myself to finding out in five seconds.

I could feel the look on Brent's face as he stared at me, mouth wide open with nothing coming out, eyes bulging in disbelief.

The Lincoln slowed to below twenty miles per hour. Seeing that the left ramp at the waterline was open, I opened my door, letting that power steering veer the classic car to the left and down the boat launch entry, the wooden ramps just ahead of us. Shifting into neutral I stepped out of the car and ran along side just long enough to close my door as the tail passed by. I grabbed at the first static object I could find, a round post the thickness of a telephone pole, just as it all hit the water.

King had resumed screaming something but I couldn't quite make out what he was saying. Could have been a prayer. I watched him try to hold his expensive tool out the window as the Lincoln settled into Lake Michigan but the weight was too much to balance with one hand. It plopped into the water, out of reach. Brent crawled out the window, onto the half-submerged roof. I guess he had some convictions left after all, beating me at chicken like that. I flipped open my phone, trying to give him the impression I couldn't hear my imaginary conversation, but he just kept jumping up and down, screaming randomly. Just then I realized I had forgotten to ask Brent if he could swim.

While waiting for the connection to go through, I pointed to the little sandy beach hugging the rocks to the left of the boat launch, trying to explain to Brent that this was where I learned how to swim as a small boy. My dad fished off of the stone breakwater at the top of the mound, where he could keep watch over my siblings and me.

Brent didn't want to hear about it, cursing my parents for having ever made me. I could hear the phone on the other end pick up.

"Papo? Hey! It's Nick Danielevitczyk! Yeah!" I had to walk away from the scene; I could still make out something of what Brent was screaming out there on my roof. "Not much, how about you? Hey, my Lincoln needs a tow. I'm out in Cal Park by the boat launch. Keys are in the car." I looked back one last time. "Yeah, its open. Yeah, over to Jara's, okay? And, Papo? Bring your waders. Fishing waders."

Nikonos, a division of Nikon, makes superior underwater housing for all sorts and sizes of both 35 millimeter and digital cameras. They are, of course, on the pricey side. Most technology is. In my adventures in the warm waters of the Caribbean, I found the Canon AS-6 35 millimeter more than adequate for the non-professional. Which for some reason reminds me of a Marx brothers joke. "I took some pictures of the native girls but they weren't developed. But we're going back again in a couple a weeks!" I think that's from 'Animal Crackers'. Love those movies. You'd think an award-winning world-traveled professional like B. J. King would be prepared for anything, right? Checking my $40 dollar Swatch watch I picked up my pace, walking across the park to the field house. The morning was almost over.

In his late teens Joey Miller did what was still known back then as 'getting a girl in trouble'. It wasn't his last unplanned attempt at progeny. She wasn't one of his high school hangers-on, but I remember she was from Roseland or Kensington, a young waitress from one of the many good Italian restaurants that ran along 115th Street west of Cottage Grove back even after the white flight. Okay, so her family owned the place, all right? Once the scandal broke, her family sent her out west to stay with some cousins until after the blessed event. Families were like that back then. I guess some families are still like that. Somewhere between Springfield, Missouri and Oklahoma City the bus she was a passenger on took a dive in a ditch and she and four other passengers were killed in the crash. The accident was blamed on two blown tires. The bullets that were retrieved were from two different guns, or so the papers said at the time.

Joey Miller, as luck would have it, had an airtight alibi on the night the 'accident' occurred. He was in the drunk tank that whole weekend for causing a fight at Roma's on Commercial at 93rd Street. Seems the baked lasagna was too well done for his taste. I remember that the girl had three older brothers, with long memories, or so their eyes said at the wake I attended for her at Panozzo's Funeral parlor on East 115th Street, in old Roseland. Anne Marie Bennedetto was her name. Yeah, I remembered it. I just didn't want to say her name. A guy doesn't forget his first.

Alderman Antonio J. Coronado proudly marched out of the City Council chambers followed by a pack of backslapping colleagues and directly into the throng of press jammed into a small hallway that lead away from the chamber and into an enlarged interview room. Shouts and whistling and applause could be heard coming from the chamber, the press calls rising above the din.

"ALDERMAN! ALDERMAN!" "Do you REALLY think your proposal has any real chance?" "ALDERMAN! What about the committee to?" "ALDERMAN! Do the voters of your ward?" Pick me! "What did the mayor mean by?" No, pick me! I'm live on camera! "ALDERMAN! Does the state legislature?" Can't you see my hand waving in your face, Alderman? "ALDERMAN!" Antonio had been plotting and planning and reliving this moment in his head for more than a decade. Now he was going to make every look and every tilt of that thick close-cropped mass of black hair on his head count.

"I stand by what I said on the council floor not ten minutes ago, as do my colleagues gathered here with me!" The alderman and his cabal had made their way behind a carefully placed podium, flanked by flags of our country, state, city and the vets flag, with the city seal prominently hung directly behind. The campaign season never ends in Chicago.

"This mayor and this administration have had the time and the opportunity again and again to improve the lives of every citizen in our great city!" The press was still jockeying for position, everybody and their camera trying to be in the front row center. But the event was SRO. "And time and again they have failed!" Coronado continued.

"Sending our proposal to committee changes nothing! We will move on this proposal because that is what our constituents want for their future and the future of generations to come on the southeast side! INDEPENDENCE!"

Coronado threw his fists into the air. Cheers and applause went up in the room, drowning out the stymied press. Reporters continued to call out questions over the noise as the aldermen congratulated themselves and posed for photographs as if this was some kind of graduation day. Crowds bussed in from the southeast side neighborhoods specifically for this 'spontaneous' occasion added to the commotion as they had fifteen minutes before from the galleries in the council chambers.

The seasoned reporters who actually had heads on their shoulders and faces for radio followed Coronado out into the larger second floor hallway leading across the elevator lobby towards the aldermanic offices. They were the guys who wrote the stories under the headlines; the ones movies got made about. The alderman let them gather close in.

"First of all, I want and need to acknowledge the deep personal loss I feel at the passing of a great city servant and close advisor to my ward. Joseph Miller was a Chicago original and will be deeply missed by all who knew him and worked with him."

"Alderman, what about the reports that a substantial sum of money was found with Miller's body? As much as twenty-five thousand dollars?" It was Justin Smith from the Chicago Today newspaper, distinguished dean of the local press corps. It was rumored he had worked with reporters who had worked with Carl Sandburg personally, back in the day. I wonder if you know who Carl Sandburg was and his connection to Chicago? No, he was not in the original 'Our Gang' comedies.

Coronado had a slightly quizzical look on his face to the stated dollar amount, which disappeared in an instant. Apparently fifteen thousand dollars did, too.

"I have not as yet spoken directly with the investigators assigned to the case since I was first informed of the situation this morning," the alderman responded. "It remains an ongoing investigation at the moment."

Arthur Josslyn, another local mainstay from the Daily News, held his recorder between himself and the alderman. "What about the Inspector General's findings on Miller's involvement with the street gangs in your ward, Alderman?" Coronado didn't care for the question, almost glaring at Josslyn.

"I could not speak directly about the findings, Arthur, as the IG's office has not yet released the report in its entirety. I will not address any alleged leaks from that office." Curt.

"Let me just say this," Coronado continued, "I am as disturbed as anyone is in this city about how Joseph Miller lost his life last night and I support the efforts of the Chicago Police Department in their search for his killer. Thank you gentlemen, and lady." Coronado had just noticed Holly Goldsmith, investigative reporter for the City News Bureau, who had saddled in with the others. He broke from the small group and walked towards the elevators.

"Alderman! I have a follow-up question to ask, if you don't mind." Goldsmith was tailing him to the just opened express elevator, the globe above the door lit in the 'up' position. Shaking his head, Coronado shrugged his shoulders and held the door open for her as she entered.

"Yes, Miss Goldsmith?" Crisp and businesslike. The doors slid closed.

Off the first floor lobby of City Hall there is a small, dark cubicle of a room where the sergeant-at-arms maintains security for the city side of the building. Banks of monitors line the rear wall of the cramped space, once actually a broom closet. Two rows of the monitors follow the interior security of the elevators in this wing of the building. Unnoticed by the officers on desk duty outside the doorway who were answering questions for lost tourists, one monitor showed the occupants of one elevator off to the side mauling each other against the wall like the opening of some European adult flick. The woman appeared to have dropped something on the floor, getting into a kneeling position. Only a passing police lieutenant caught the noontime tryst in black and white. Stopping to greet the two desk officers, Vic Hanley made his way towards the low-rise elevators, headed to the fifth floor, but then changed his direction.

─────────

Built in 1926, the Calumet Park field house had recently undergone extensive repair work to bring it back from the edge of demolition. Some of the exterior renovations were continuing. Stepping under some scaffolding, I pulled open the heavy metal and glass double doors and asked myself how many times I had done this since childhood.

Entering the lobby I gave a nod to the glass case-enclosed wooden schooner, 'Whisper' to my right and wondered if its long-gone artisan builders had ever floated it out in open waters. The sound of broken glass brought me back to the here and now. It came from inside the museum to my left.

The gates were open and the lights were on. I entered the James P. Fitzgibbons Museum where the Southeast Chicago Historical Society had held the fort since 1985. They outgrew the once spacious room in the mid-'90's but kept stuffing and cataloging every artifact, book, family photograph collection and odd and end pertaining to the southeast side that came through the doors. Joann Podkul Murphy was holding a dustbin over the garbage can, pouring in another load of broken glass. She saw me enter.

"Where have you been? Did you bring the doughnuts?" I shook my head. They were in the back seat of the Lincoln. Maybe Brent was living off of them by now, waiting for the rescue party.

"It's been a morning out there."

"Here too. Go look." Joann nodded her head towards the sidewall where a few other members were gathered. "Nick's here!" she announced. "No doughnuts!" Did these people not have their own ride to Calumet Bakery?

"Forgot the doughnuts, huh?" Kevin Murphy kidded me. Joann was his better half. He was a legitimate author. And historian. And a couple of other things I couldn't remember. Kind of a complete renaissance man. Also very heavy and because of such, not in the best of health.

"Morning, Kevin. Morning Alex. Frank. Now what's this?" I was referring to the obviously smashed glass display case against the wall, the remnants of which the boys were cleaning up. Boys. Not one under seventy-five. Frank Capra would have cast every one of them in his classics.

"This is what Ora and I found this morning when we opened up," Frank Stanley said. Retired out of South Works. Quiet type, steel trap for a memory and the driest sense of wit you never wanted to go up against. "The police were in and we made a report and they took their photographs. Kind of exciting!"

"So what's missing?" asked Alex Savestano, eldest among the irregulars. Lifelong southeast sider, retired out of International Harvester before its collapse in 1980. Organized the monthly senior bus trips up to Wrigley Field during the summer months. I liked him a lot anyway. Yes, I'm an out and proud White Sox fan. "Anybody have a clue?"

Frank reached into the case for the remaining treasures on display. "Let's at least get everything else out of here before there's more damage." Alex helped. The flat-topped glass case was the resting place of an impressive collection of helmets, from the World Wars forward.

"Kevin, didn't you take shots inside here last month for the open house?" Joann had walked up to join us. "Maybe you can piece together what all was on display." The other end of the glass case had contained a small collection of memorabilia and ephemera from the Century of Progress Exhibition, 1933-34, I recalled to myself. On loan from a friend of mine, Polish Jay. I didn't want to spoil their hunt so I kept shut. "What do you think, Nick?"

Frank and Alex carried the artifacts over to the large round table in the southeast corner of the room. It was where we all ended up every Wednesday for our unscheduled meeting. I took a slow look at the damage and surrounding area.

"You're on the right track, but if I may, what's missing is not from the cabinet." I pointed to the blank space about eight feet above the smashed case. "I'd like to know what was hanging there until recently. Something heavy, by the look of the remaining screws."

"Kevin, did you guys hear that?" They hadn't. "Nick wants to know what was hanging up here, above the cabinet." Joann pointed to the blank space, a pair of large side-by-side screws still embedded in the plaster wall. I checked the floor and area across from the smashed cabinet. Everything was as crowded as usual, file boxes under old sewing machines parked next to more glass cabinets filled with neighborhood remnants and treasures. Nothing old/new had rolled into the space. Whatever was on the wall fell during the theft. Or the thief's foot had gone through the case.

"You making up for not bringing the doughnuts, Nick?" Alex could be quite the kidder, too.

"No doughnuts!?" a flabbergasted Ora Coon said from the doorway, carrying a glass pot by its orange handle with both of her small, aged hands. "What am I supposed to do with all this coffee?" She had been the treasurer of the society since the doors opened. A retired librarian, this place was to her, like the others, their life contribution to their community.

━━━━━━━━━━

Lieutenant Victor Hanley leaned over a counter in some sterile, sub-basement office in the bowels of City Hall, patiently awaiting the return of the clerk-technician with his requested item. His trademark ashtray and lighter were on the counter, with a pair of cigarette butts already stamped out. The sound of the young, male, bespectacled clerk-tech's shoes could be heard echoing his return. Somewhere in the distance elevator music was softly playing a Mantovani-like tune. He handed the Lieutenant a small, square package, about the size of a CD jewel box. Hanley handed the clerk-tech paperwork attached to a clipboard, which he read, signed and returned to the lieutenant. A legally binding confidentiality agreement. Vic exited the office, emptying his ashtray in a convenient wastebasket at the swinging door before pocketing his treasures. He could be heard whistling along with the music.

A large black limousine with the license plate number '10' pulled out of the driveway of the Cardinal's traditional residence on North State Parkway in the Gold Coast neighborhood, headed back downtown to City Hall. A woman's work is never done.

━━━━━━━━━━

After monitoring the WGN News midday broadcast for the top stories, all of them local, a rarity in itself, Joann switched off the black and white portable and we got down to business.

"Does anybody feel more independent today than they did yesterday?" Alex asked. That got a good laugh from the crowd. "I sure don't!"

"I don't remember asking anybody to move me out of town!" Kevin countered. They were going to have their fun.

"Its just politics. It ain't gonna happen," Frank asserted. "Just noise for the next election."

"Frank's right," I had to jump in. "Coronado is smart enough to know he and three other aldermen aren't enough to get this pushed through the council. So what he's really up to is politics. Here I am, Mr. Mayor! Watch out!"

"Where does that leave the southeast side?" Joann brought it back home. Joann Podkul Murphy was one of those genuine joys to know in the community, and a non-stop advocate for the expansion of parkland and preserves in the Calumet area, as was her husband. She may have even been called a tree hugger every so often.

Except for the occasional dedication ceremony, (camera opportunity), City Hall occupants from outside the southeast side rarely ventured here, elections excluded, of course. And if it weren't for the vote count, the southeast side would remain a suburb of Chicago in the minds of politicians who treated it like one for generations. Oh yeah, and the tax revenue. We get the stripes for the bike lanes and the reduced lanes for actual traffic, but have you ever tried to walk from Commercial Avenue eastbound along 100th Street, or along 106th Street west of the Calumet River bridge? Bad enough by day but don't try either at night. Neither stretch has been repaired since the Great Depression, and they look it. Pride of place, huh? I guess the pedestrian vote doesn't count for much anymore. Where, oh where will we stick another bike rental pavilion?

"Wasn't it some kind of trophy?" Alex got the train of thought off of the political tracks.

"I think you have something there," Frank admitted. "Where're the mini-Battlin' Nelson gloves?" I stepped over to the cabinet and checked behind the case.

"They're here on the floor behind the cabinet. What were they hanging from?" I asked. Ora brought over the broom to edge them out from behind.

"The sixty-four thousand dollar question!" Alex joked. My phone rang. It was my tow guy. Everybody had a laugh, as Ora reached for the tip jar and passed it in my general direction. All phones needed to be set on 'vibrate' after entering the museum, otherwise the guilty owner had to feed a dollar into the jar, for future coffee supplies. I tipped the jar and flipped open my phone, rising and walking towards the exit.

"Hey Papo! Did you find it alright?" A pause. "Well, just save the ticket for me and drag it over to Jara's. I'll get it from there later, thanks!" Another pause. "Just tell the police he was a stowaway. No, I'm not paying anybody to dredge the lake bottom for camera gear, he's on his own. G'bye!" I hesitated to return to the judgment table.

"Car problems?" Frank inquired.

"Naw, since they demolished Skyway Car Wash to make a parking lot for that new school I haven't found a good detail shop I'm happy with."

Alex felt obliged to add, "Welcome to the club!" Everybody shared a laugh on me, the youngest guy in the room.

"It's not a trophy. It's that bell!" announced Kevin, holding a print from his photos of the open house. "See in the background behind Joe Mulac? That's the ship's bell we got from the American

Shipyard when it closed. I think it was off of the steamship William E. Corey. See the long rope with all those knots underneath?"

"Well, I thought it was something metallic," Alex added.

"I think the shipyard closed when Buchanan was alderman," Frank remembered.

"Who would want to break in here to steal a bell?" Ora wanted to know. I stepped behind Kevin to get a look at the photograph. Consciously, I reached into my shirt pocket and lifted out my reading glasses, to see if I would recognize that rope. You know that feeling in the pit of your stomach?

"Now we can let the police know and they can get to it!" Joann said with a firmness that meant business. Several thoughts ran through me as I grasped the print, having seen another image of that same oddly knotted rope earlier in the day. A capture I had caused to be destroyed.

———

The black limo of the Alderman of the 10th Ward of the City of Chicago pulled to a stop back in front of his office on south Commercial Avenue, parking just behind the now empty people mover. Antonio Coronado exited, while the driver manned the rear door. Antonio seemed a bit put off that none of the hired 'spontaneous' crowd had stuck around after they were brought back from the downtown show, to greet his return. Neither had the most recent swarm of press. Checking his watch, he let it pass and entered the stairwell. The chauffer returned to his chores, driving the matriarch to her nearby home in South Shore.

Coronado walked into the office area and, ignoring the greetings from the secretarial pool, walked directly into Erlinda's office. She looked up as Tony closed the door.

"That went well!" Lynn said, switching off a flat screen TV on the wall.

"My mother suggests we move the cash out of here for a while. I tend to agree with her." Tony said, above a whisper.

Erlinda thought to herself "Of course you do." but instead asked, "Where did she have in mind?"

"Nothing definite." Not quite genuinely spontaneous, "Do you think we could stash it at your place?"

"No Tony, and it's not my place." He accepted the answer as final.

"I don't think it's a good idea to keep it here overnight. Not with the mayor's boys on the warpath."

"And your home isn't safe? For the money, I mean."

"Nah, this is coming down quick and large!" He sat down. "How heavy do you think it is? I mean, all of it?"

"I couldn't carry it all in one load. I don't suppose the boys next door could, either." She was trying to be helpful without being too helpful. Lynn knew a situation when she smelled it, and had been worried about all that cash in one place since it was first revealed to her as a small fortune when she had started work as the alderman's private secretary. It had grown considerably.

"I don't doubt Joey told the goons all about it when he put it together up here, but they would have been out the door already if they had the combination," he said half to himself. "Remind me to fire those two knuckleheads next week after all this dies down. Okay. Here's what I want done with the campaign contributions."

━━━━━━━

Mid afternoon when the group of irregulars broke up, I walked west from the field house, through some undergrowth (inner city forest for the uninitiated) and north along the single set of railroad tracks that border Calumet Park. This line still services Iroquois Landing and across the Calumet River, the former site of South Works.

I ended up at Jara's Auto at 96th and Ewing, where my four-wheel yacht was still in the works, so I decided to take a walk over to Polish Jay's to kill time. I was hungry, too. No doughnuts will do that. Walking under the railroad viaduct on Ewing, I remembered seeing the museum's collection of antique photos of the depot that stood at street level here, just about where the Skyway continues its descent from the bridge southeast and into Indiana. The other side of the street, where a tank stands today, was the Host House from the

Century of Progress. Route 41 and Indianapolis Boulevard was a major pathway for travelers to the fair from the east.

I passed by the latest football squad from de Sales, dressed in full gear, walking over to Cal Park for their daily workout. Not my alma mater, but they brought back memories just the same. I had to step off the sidewalk to clear the way for the tight ends who didn't bother to look up from their smart phones. I took a soft left onto the boulevard and stopped at Route 66 for a quick slice of pizza. A satisfying walking meal in itself.

Polish Jay's place was an old, brick barn, built in 1914 as a commercial wood shop, just a short walk east from the Calumet River. Many of the existing houses in the neighborhood had their wood trimming and framing cut here, a century ago. It had always reminded me of a shy turtle, the building jutting out almost to the sidewalk, the curved roofline resembling the top shell. I remember coming here as a boy with Dad, for dry ice and fire extinguisher refills. Grant Hagberg had the place then. The outside hadn't changed much, but I doubt if old man Hagberg would recognize the inside now, or his formerly truck-filled backyard that once included a ten-ton dry ice machine.

I bypassed the front door, which entered into an office space, and walked down the driveway just north of the structure to the back building, well, a pile of shipping containers actually, that Jay had had constructed when he struck it rich. I rang a concealed doorbell, and admired the nasturtiums and vines growing from the top of the wall, the afternoon sunlight making the lengthy cobblestone driveway resemble some European village gateway.

"I was expecting you, Nick." It was Jay speaking from up above, leaning over the metal railing of the apartment's second floor. "Hang on a minute." I could hear him coming down the metal steps and unlocking the high wood gate with its distinctive rounded top, like something out of 'The Hobbit' that opened out onto the driveway. "A lot of people are interested in you today. C'mon in!" Smiling, he shook my hand warmly.

Jay led the way into an atrium garden, complete with a meandering koi pond that ended farther to the right at the sunken hot tub, looking like a shaky exclamation point from above. We headed up the steps parallel to the pond, to the balcony on top of a single stack container.

"Take a gander at the activity on the river." Jay handed me his binoculars. His cell phone rang. It was the 'Jeopardy' theme song. Appropriate, since that was where Polish Jay had won his fortune some years back.

"744. Must be the police. Again." Some emphasis on that last word. "Hello." Jay stepped inside his apartment. I focused the binoculars westward, looking at the white evidence tent that had popped up on the east side of the Calumet River, a couple of police vehicles on site with it. The backlit effect of the afternoon sunlight on the scene gave it an ominous glow. Maybe it was just the heat, but the personnel on hand appeared to be moving in slow motion.

"You better check in with the police, Nicky. They think you went down with the ship!" Jay had stepped back onto the balcony.

I was nonplussed. "It's okay, they're watching your place, too."

"What?"

"Here, look for yourself." I handed Jay his binoculars to check out the police with sets of their own, looking at the pair of us on the balcony, watching them. "I wonder what Brent told them?" I asked.

"B. J. King in the 'hood? I should have him sign some of his prints I picked up on eBay," Jay joked.

It suddenly dawned on me that I'd left the phone on 'silent' hours ago and hadn't switched the ring tone back on. I also noticed the battery had run out.

"D'you think we should wave 'hello' to the police?" Jay wondered aloud.

"I'll call them back from home." I returned the dead phone to my pocket. "I hope you got those pictures for a song!"

"No such luck! They're from the set he won the prize for. You were a lot thinner back then!" Jay put the binoculars down. "We're going to have company."

"And you still had hair!" Jay was as bald as a cue ball. "You know I never did sign the release for those shots. Buoscio talked me out of suing him and the News. Effing public domain, they said!" Jay put a hand on my shoulder. "I guess I won't have to bother with that call from home."

"Yeah, saving those three kids from that fire was a real private moment for you!" He was smiling that big, dumb grin of his. Up to his eyes it went. "Want a drink before you go, firewalker?" I had to laugh.

"Some headline! They even spelled my name right for the last time!" I joined Jay's smile. "How about a cold water?"

"Coming up!" Jay stepped back into his apartment. I heard a splash coming from the koi pond, and followed the progress of a large speckled fish swimming away from the wake. "How do your fish handle the heat?"

"They get a couple of buckets of ice every day and pray I never get hold of a good recipe for fish-head soup!" Jay handed over a perfectly chilled bottle of water, not the cheap stuff but the kind that burps when you crank it open. "You still hear from those kids?"

Ignoring the question, I took the bottle from Jay and pressed it to my forehead. "Thanks, I needed that!"

"So, why are they looking at you for Joey Miller's murder? You were here last night. Have you spoken with a lawyer?"

"I'm a popular choice and no, not since Ron died." I corrected myself. "Except for Jerry, but that's different." There was a loud knock at the gate below us. I looked over the railing. "Detective Sasuta, I presume?"

———

Avoiding any hint of controversy was something the Catholic Archdiocese in Chicago was well known for, though admitting its own sins to its congregants was another matter. A two-line notice was sent via fax to all the local news outlets. Nothing like keeping up with technology, which may explain why a number of local television stations hadn't gotten the news until their producers saw the announcement made on other channels. Yes, they do watch each other. Constantly.

A press release later that evening read: "The Archdiocese of Chicago will perform a funeral mass at Immaculate Conception

Church for Joseph A. Miller, late of South Chicago, to be followed by internment at Holy Sepulchre cemetery in Alsip, Illinois. This at the request of his family and friends." Between the lines it should have added: At the intervention of one Angela Maria Serros-Coronado.

———

The ride to the Calumet Area police headquarters and court building on East 111th Street in Pullman was uneventful, and mostly silent, after the two detectives introduced themselves. They were not who I was expecting, but rather were the pair assigned to the Leon Perez murder case. Other than background, I wasn't exactly sure why I was in the back seat of their unmarked police vehicle. The molded plastic seat was uncomfortable and a little sticky in spots. Also, there were no seat belts. Back here.

If you've seen any 'Law & Order' episodes broadcast over the last 25 years, you already know what the inside of an 'interview room' looks like: metal door with a narrow, vertical window; cinder block walls; metal furniture and a one-way glass window or two. Add bad lighting, poor choice of color for the paint on the walls, no real art except for some initials and crude remarks carved into the top of the desk from some long past occupant or two.

What you don't get from the TV screen is the experience of being led into one of these rooms and left to fend for yourself while the detectives hob knob with their colleagues and superiors before beginning the interrogation. And if you're in this room make no mistake, this will be an interrogation. TV also leaves out the clammy feeling on your skin, the sweet, antiseptic smell of cleaning solution used to mop up the place and the noises your stomach invariably makes when it is least appropriate to do so.

I heard a door slam out in the hallway and a slight rattling sound of the one-way window from the effect. The conference with the unseen behind the looking glass was at an end. The door opened.

"Sorry to keep you waiting, I'm sure you have better things to do today," said Detective Rocky J. Ungard, the lead dick on this case. He looked a few months shy of retirement himself, on the short side, but a bit stocky in the shoulders and slim in the waist, with wisps of

Grecian-formula tinted hair on his otherwise balding head. I later found out he was a past Golden Gloves winner in the 1960's, originally from Chicago's west side. He didn't look like the kind of cop who put up with much of anything.

Ungard's partner was a young, quite attractive Black woman, Traci Ducree. She hadn't rolled far from the apple tree herself, having lived in Roseland her entire life. Her very good looks were probably her best weapon in this job. I found out later she was third generation in uniform.

"Not a problem, detective," I replied. "Glad to help out if I can."

"We just want to understand your involvement with the deceased is all, Mr. – " he checked a manila file he had carried in with him and tried to pronounce my last name without actually speaking. That did not seem to work.

"Daniels is fine, sir." I tried to help him off the hook.

"Danielevitchia – Dan –" the detective seemed determined to master my last name. His partner was silent. She had sat down when they entered the room and was just watching me. I glanced between the two of them while Ungard paced the room. "Daniels," he gave up, closing the file and eyeing me from a standing position. "Were you two, you know?" he gave me a knowing, disapproving look, and a wave of his free hand.

I was wondering when the floorshow would be over. "Are you asking if we were lovers, sir?" I shot back an incredulous look, mostly for his partner's benefit.

"Perez was a known homosexual in the community, according to his file." Ungard held up another manila folder. "It's all right here." He placed the files on the table, patting them down for emphasis.

"For the record, detective, Leon was bisexual, he did not keep that a secret, and he was married, to women, twice. I'm not sure how legal it is to gather that kind of information you have on any individual in the twenty-first century, but I am sure that being bisexual, or even being gay in this town is no longer illegal, even way down here."

"Really? Since I walked into this room five minutes ago you haven't checked me out once, and I've been told I'm quite beautiful."

It was Detective Ducree. She stood and took a walk around the table to prove the point. What in the hell were these two up to? "Maybe I'm just not your type, Mr. Daniels?"

Ungard had sat down, and now he was watching me. "We know there is a secret circle of this kind of activity in the community, Daniels," Ungard leaned slightly into the table, "and all we're trying to determine is, who is who and what is what. For the record." That last crack was for my earlier jibe. I really hate it when cops go out of their way to stereotype themselves.

"Do you guys own a calendar in this precinct?" I had to ask without laughing. "That's a joke, Detective Ducree, not any indication of gender bias on my part." Was it getting warm in here?

"Comedy may not be your strong suit, Mr. Daniels. If you're some kind of all-American hetero-male, why would you provide a location for some other kind of sexual activity, if you didn't personally support it?" She seemed determined to get my pants off one way or another, leaning over me from behind, breathing down my neck.

"He hadn't worked for weeks according to his file, so how much was Perez paying you in rent for the apartment?" Ungard had me there.

"Nothing."

"Nothing?" Ungard seemed mortified. "Were you taking it out in some sort of trade, Daniels?"

"Seems more likely the decedent had something on you, doesn't it?" Ducree had a one-track mind. I had to control myself or I'd start to sweat in this box.

"Leon was my friend. He needed a place to stay. I had an empty apartment."

"Yes and about that apartment. Wasn't some other crime committed there just about a year ago?" Ungard enjoyed his work. I guess he had memorized my file, as he hadn't opened the folder since that first time after entering the room. "Something involving a military man?"

"You do seem to attract a certain element of the populace, Mr. Daniels," Ducree purred, or was that my imagination?

I leaned back in the metal chair, which was less comfortable than when I first sat down, and had to give a small laugh at myself. "Neither one of these detectives," I put some emphasis on that last word, slowly standing, "has yet to ask me one question that might actually help in their investigation of my friend's murder. Are any of you shadows behind the curtain interested in that?"

After a pause someone in the next room knocked on the glass twice.

The black limo pulled away from the offices of the Alderman of the 10th Ward of the City of Chicago, for the short ride back to his modest home in Hegewisch. A few members of his office staff were also exiting the building, ending their workday. Upstairs, in the large meeting room, surrounded by the forest of floral tributes, a number of precinct captains were reading the cards attached to the flowers, remarking at the distance some had been sent from. Some were from businesses and individuals with organization connections, names familiar to anyone who read a newspaper or a police bulletin in the last 20 years. Up against a wall, one oversized tribute was in the shape of a lucky horseshoe, with the open end on top. No card was attached, but the banner read "*Via Con Dios Pendejo*".

Further inside the space and behind the French doors where Joey Miller had his modest public office set up, Eduardo Z and Bernard P were concerned with other matters.

"Nobody's returning my calls, man!" Bernard checked his watch. "I don't unnerstand." Bernard looked a lot older than the given age on his driver's license. All those shots and beers and whatever. His hair had maintained its color from high school, a hue of straw and the texture to match that had to be generational. The mullet cut completed the image. "They said they'd call, right? Am I right?" It was a small space to be pacing inside of, but he did his best to use all the carpet.

"I don't get none of it," Eduardo said with a dismissive wave of his hand. The close-cropped, jet-black hair on his head belied the fact that he and Bernard were the same age. He looked 10 years younger than his pacing partner. He had always come across as the brains of the triad; just submissive to the thug who, until yesterday, had occupied the chair Eduardo was now getting uncomfortably used to. "Why don't you go out for a drink?"

Bernard turned and looked at him. "Not until we know what's what. This weren't no part of any plan I heard of, Lalo! Tony didn't even come in here once! Nothin'!"

"I think the plan has changed for us, B. The day is done and our own cops aren't checking in tells you something, I'm just sayin'."

"So we sit here and wait for what?"

"The office girls are outta here so we go next door and get some funds and ride." Eduardo held up a yellowed piece of paper.

"That's the plan?"

Eduardo unfolded the paper to reveal a series of numbers. "I'm sayin' there is no plan, B. This is what we got. The cops ain't callin' 'cuz they're not in my pocket or yours, man. They got emancipated on the beach this morning. We stick around here and they're lookin' at us for this, B!"

Bernard thought for a long moment. "Let's close up like any given Wednesday and blow this pop stand."

Shaking his head, Eduardo shut off the desk light and started toward the French doors. Bernard doubled back and reached under the desk for something that made a muffled clanking sound when he picked it up. Eduardo opened both doors wide and walked out with Bernard a close second. "Let's move."

"Aren't you gonna lock it?" Bernard asked.

"What for?"

They exited the space but were met by a few leftovers from the day's work. Erlinda was just locking the outer office door, talking with Steve and Elsie Gaddus, elderly precinct workers from the East Side.

Eduardo wasn't crazy for the small crowd of witnesses. "Hey! Excuse me, Lynn? Lynn? Could I talk a minute wit' you?" Bernard lagged behind, and thinking about what he was carrying, started for the stairs.

"Yes, Eduardo?" She didn't step away from the couple and they seemed set to wait for her. "The alderman has left for the day and we're closing up now."

"I wuz just gonna ask if I could speak wit' you a minute in private, about the situation and all, is all."

"Well, as I said, the alderman has already left for the day and any discussion about the day's situation would have to go through him, of course. I know it's been a rough one for you, well, for all of us, but you understand, the alderman will have to handle the details for the time being." She knew exactly what he wanted to really talk about. "Goodnight, Eduardo." That sounded kind but final, and Lynn turned her attention to the two aged captains.

"Right. G'night. G'night everybody." Eduardo nodded to the Gadduses and walked down the staircase to the street, waiting for the door to close behind him. "That bitch!"

"What'd she say?" Bernard was returning from their car parked up the street. "What?"

"Fuckin' bitch, man! Let's come back later after we eat." They walked to their black muscle car parked in front of the building to their left, where Bernard had deposited the weighty item he had been carrying. Neither one noticed the unmarked police car across the street, parked in front of Steel City Furniture. They also didn't notice the man behind the wheel taking notes.

"Where we goin'?"

"Skyway Dogs, man! Take my mind off that bitch!" Their car pulled out into traffic as the last three people exited the Fink Building for the night.

Erlinda locked the front door. The unmarked police car made a u-turn and pulled up directly in front of the doorway. Erlinda waved a 'thank you' to the officer in the driver's seat and walked north along Commercial Avenue with the Gadduses. The street looked better at dusk when the city lights were just warming up, than at any other time of the day. Except maybe in the first light of morning.

Antonio Coronado sat in his living room, a late edition newspaper across his lap, his cell phone at his ear. Listening. Lydia was in the kitchen, finishing the dinner dishes. Their children were in the backyard playing. The front door bell rang.

"I got it!" Tony announced, as he stepped to the door, still listening to the one-way conversation on his phone. Lydia stepped into the dining room, wiping a dish dry while trying to see who was at the front door this late. Tony snapped on the front porch light. It was Vic Hanley.

"Good evening, Alderman."

"Let me call you back." Tony ended the call. "Hey Vic, thanks for the coverage today." Opening the screen door, he extended his hand and shook the lieutenant's. "Did you want to stop in for a beer?"

"No, I'm headed home myself. Just wanted to check in with you and be sure my men were out front. Lotta fireworks today."

"More to follow!" Antonio laughed. "G'night, Vic. And thanks again."

"Good night, Alderman." Hanley walked down the steps from the front door and stepped over to the two uniformed officers in the squad parked out front, leaning into the passenger side window.

"You boys keep awake out here, now."

"Yes sir." They answered in unison.

"Need anything call the precinct and here's my card if there are any overnight incidents." Vic patted the arm of the officer in the passenger seat and stepped back to his own vehicle. The two Black officers looked at each other.

"Cracker!" said the driver, shaking his head.

"Maybe, but I need the overtime," responded the passenger.

―――――――――

Eduardo Z sat at the counter just out of eyesight of the order windows inside Skyway Dog House. The milkshake mixer machine was going full blast out of view. Night was coming on fast as he watched the traffic on Ewing Avenue pass by, some cars with headlights blazing, others saving their batteries.

"The street lights are on stupid! Don'cha know enough to turn on your lights? Don'cha know the law, wetback?" Eduardo said to no one in particular as he waited for Bernard to bring the food over from the window to the counter. "Don' forget my shake!"

Bernard shrugged his shoulders as if to say, "I'm not makin' the stuff! Hold on!" Eating here was a ritual with these two knuckleheads. Even in high school this was their hangout place, when they weren't 'busy' with Joey Miller, or into their own brands of extreme mischief. Real second story kind of guys, or so said the rumor mill.

"Number 71!" the girl inside the window opening called out. Bernard passed over the ticket stub with the number 71 printed in red on it and helped himself to extra napkins. He stepped over to the counter and grabbed up the red plastic oval bowls containing their orders of hot dogs and fries.

"Damn!' Bernard half-whispered. "We just missed getting her to say '69'!" and laughed.

"Get the shakes, man! You let 'em sit there and get watery every time!" Eduardo ordered, and had a laugh as Bernard complied. "69! Shit!"

"Dig in, dog!"

"I am, Cuz!"

The pair ate their meal, checking out the cars riding by and the customers picking up their dinners.

After we got down to business, the interrogation did become an interview. The chief of detectives for the district was one of the shadows behind the glass and got Ungard and Ducree off the sex track and onto something more substantial. They were most interested in the stolen bell from the historical society museum, and summoned the police who had done the initial on site investigation, along with the rope from the crime scene. Being in the same room with the weapon that was used to murder my friend was a bit much, but I managed to stay cool, outside. Inside I wanted a few minutes with the animal that ended Leon.

At the end of the interview, Detective Ducree walked me over to the desk she shared with her partner and let me use her phone, a desk model straight out of the '70's. I could tell which side of the desk was hers by the tidiness and family photos. She wanted to walk me out of the building but I assured her I already knew the way out and I was glad to use it. That parting smile of hers was memorable, but not in any confidence-building way.

As I neared the blessed exit to the modern, sterile, weirdly colored 11th district police headquarters, I spotted two of the boys who had found Joey's body floating off of the coast of Black Beach. They were seated on a bench off to one side, clinging tightly to their parents. I recognized the boys from Brent's captures, and the morning's television coverage of the riverside event. All of them looked like they had seen better days.

"*Via con Dios, ninos!*" I said as I walked past them and out the door. I wanted to glance back to see their parents' reaction, but I didn't. I did notice the pretty, young woman with reddish brown hair, seated on a bench to the side of the boys. I didn't know her, though.

I waited outside the headquarters near the curb on East 111th Street. A familiar car pulled up. "Thanks," I said as I opened the car door and jumped inside.

"Would you prefer we keep the air conditioning going?" Lynn asked. I couldn't quite tell if she was mad or just tired from the political grind she had to put up with from her brother-in-law. I think the day had been long enough for a lot of people.

"Whatever you like, babe." She smiled and left the windows rolled up. "You hungry?"

"Look in the back." As we passed under a street lamp I could make out a large Capri's Pizza box looking lonely and delicious on the back seat.

"Somebody loves me!"

"That's not all for you, you know!" She was smiling but kept her eyes on the road.

"I should have smelled the aroma when I got in. Must be getting old."

"You better not be getting old! Not tonight, anyway!"

"Have you got plans for the evening?" She just continued to smile. Somebody did love me.

After we polished off the best pizza in the neighborhood and a couple of beers to wash it all down, I headed upstairs for a quick shower before bed. The day had been long and hard enough. I stepped into the rounded corner shower stall and was refreshed by the thick, warm sheets of water. I had to mentally congratulate myself again for sinking the money into remodeling the bathroom first, even if it did put me in debt. I couldn't shake the image of that rope out of my head. I wondered if Brent had mentioned my destroying his images of it to the police yet? It didn't matter. I was sure the forensics crew got enough captures of their own for everybody's satisfaction.

My mind was occupied with other things when I noticed two very soft hands soaping up my back. Lynn pressed in behind me and closed the curved sliding door.

"Good thing this fits two!" I said over the sound of the water as I turned around.

"Hey! I wasn't done with that side." Lynn pressed her face to my wet chest. I guess we weren't as tired as we thought we were.

━━━━━━━━━━

A familiar black muscle car pulled to a stop across the street from the Fink Building, idling. After a moment or two the occupants slowly rolled forward and continued northbound on Commercial Avenue. The officer in the unmarked police car parked directly in front of the building made a note of the time.

THURSDAY

I woke up feeling too good to be bothered with Joey Miller, at least for one day.

The windows in our second floor bedroom were open and fresh cool night air off the lake had left a kind of crispness after the dawn. As was her habit since moving in, whenever she could Lynn left without waking me. She had made coffee, I could smell the aroma coming from the kitchen downstairs, wafting up through this old house, my money pit. I stared at the ceiling, still too content to get out of the bed. I got up anyway, but with no immediate agenda, I ended up parading around the house naked for the better part of an hour before I bothered to dress. My only real regret from yesterday was losing Leon. Which only produced angry thoughts about his demise at the end of a rough life and my damned interrogation the night before at the Calumet PHQ. And maybe just a little regret about that scathing obit-blog I sent in to the Service. Perhaps I got lucky and Larry didn't include it in the overnight posting.

By nine I was on the road.

While doing research for a story on the gangs of South Chicago a number of years back, I came across a book in the South Chicago branch library. In it was where I first met Leon Perez, including photos that were taken of him by the author, in the 1980's. Leon was a member of the Latin Counts street gang. As several copies of the book had already been stolen from the library, the branch manager let me know the volume was only available as a reference book, so I had to read it then and there, making notes. I eventually found a used copy on the Internet. Larry also made one available in the Calumet News office. In the text and photographs Leon was a highlight of the seventh chapter, titled "Make The Angels Cry".

Growing up in the area, I knew kids who were gang members. Everybody our age knew someone who was, or had a cousin or friend or even a brother, who belonged to a gang. Membership transcended race, creed or color, even the financial separation of the classes. It came with the territory and the times, so everybody thought.

By the time I had tracked him down, life had taken an odder than expected turn for Leon. He was living in the southwest suburbs in somewhat shabby conditions, performing day work, sometimes dressed up as the Statue of Liberty for a tax preparer, standing on a busy sidewalk carrying a sign and a torch. He enjoyed wearing a costume for work, which explained why his favorite holiday was Halloween. He also had worked for a few costume shops out in the 'burbs, and in his post-gang days had spent time in Job Corps, fighting forest fires, of all things.

From the first, Leon was quite candid about his past and about life in general. He couldn't believe we both attended the same high school. As a little boy, family members had given him the nickname of 'Wicho' and that stuck around for a long time, even through high school. When his younger cousin convinced him to join the street gang, Leon was tagged with the moniker 'Psycho', in part because of his wild and unpredictable behavior after sniffing a popular brand of carburetor cleaner with a pig on the label, for a cheap high. Life on the can, he called it.

The thrill of gang life was not what Leon had ever sought out, it was just another thing to do to pass the time in the 'hood. His younger cousin, who had gotten Leon violated into the gang in the first place, was later killed in a shooting a couple of blocks from the house where they both were living. There was a black and white photograph of Leon as a pallbearer at his cousin's funeral in that reference book at the library.

I walked the few blocks distance from my home to Jara's Auto Repair on Ewing Avenue, to retrieve the waterlogged Lincoln. It was parked just outside the entry ramp on the side of the building, kitty-corner from St. George's church.

"What do you do with that car Nick?" José Jara, the proprietor, wanted to know. "Papo brings it in, there are fish pouring outta the doors!" His crew let out a loud laugh from inside the shop.

I feigned looking about. "So where are my fish?"

"We had 'em for lunch!" Everybody had a good laugh at the expense of my ride. And I'm guessing, a meal on me.

Patting me on the back, José walked me through the shop and into his office. Of course he had to lead me past his 1930 black Pontiac four-door, on blocks and under a clear plastic tarp, but I knew what it was and why he had me walk past it, giving me a wink and a nod towards the classic as he held the glass door open, as if to say, "Wanna trade?"

"So you get a ticket for that joy ride yesterday?" He handed me his bill.

"No, not yet. Just this!" I held up his invoice with one hand while reaching for my wallet with the other. It wasn't so much, but I winced when I handed José the cash anyway, just to let him know that every little bit hurts. "You should try it sometime. The ride, I mean!"

And, yes, I did get an actual ticket of all things for using the Park District launch ramp without paying the launch fee! Typical Chicago!

Westbound on 95th, I drove past the two-flat, wondering if I should just sell the place now, after all the drama there. A small crowd had gathered on the sidewalk by a makeshift memorial to Leon, flowers and balloons waving in the breeze, with a large white cross for the focal point. I made a mental note to call Jerry C, a local property lawyer I knew, to get a second opinion.

About Lynn, Erlinda Sanchez, and me. We first met at some political rally I was covering for the Service, during her brother in-law's last unsuccessful campaign. We'd been seeing each other for several months and since I had acquired a big, mostly empty house, decided to move in together. Coming from a somewhat traditional background Lynn had yet to introduce me to her family at large, beyond her sister and brother-in-law. The former was a very kind though quiet young woman whose life was focused on her children; the latter, well, because of the Service I had to work with the alderman's office, now and then. We didn't have to like each other, did we? I got the feeling that he didn't 'approve' of his sister-in-law dating, and then living with, a *guero*, a white guy.

Lynn and I were quite comfortable together for the most part and I made sure that my work didn't conflict with hers. Without saying so I'm sure she did the same thing for me. Of course I should have asked if I caused her any problems with the alderman or his precinct captains and various thugs, but I kept my mouth shut about it. One of the few things I guess I did keep my mouth shut about.

Over the bridge I cut a soft right onto South Chicago Avenue. Slowing down just before the fire station, I hung a right on 93rd to avoid the Commercial Avenue traffic lights. One of the station shifts was hosing down the company engine, number 46. This house also had hook & ladder number 17 and ambulance 9. I've spent some time covering a couple of their shifts for the Service. Almost immediately I took a left, northbound on Houston. This corner, north and across the street from the firehouse, was the site of the first Bowen School, about a century before.

Just east across the street and north a couple of doors from the empty parking lot which had replaced Bowen School was the former office of the local chapter of the CIO, a very important union organization around here 90 years before, the flanking eagles above the arched doorway always grabbing my attention. Now the place housed a church, like a lot of significant buildings in the 'hood.

Turning west on 88th Street and south onto Commercial, I found a parking spot almost across the street from the office and pulled in. I waited to get out of my car while a fire engine passed, number 46 again. They didn't even get the chance to dry off their truck, I thought. I wondered how I'd survive a 24-hour shift with Chicago's bravest. Growing up to be a fireman never made the top of my future careers list when I was a kid. Of course, I never thought I'd run into a burning building, either. Go figure.

———

"Good morning, Louise!" I said as I entered the office.

"You're in a good mood this morning," she replied. "This might take the glow outta your cheeks, Nick. Mr. Larry wants to see you. Upstairs. First thing." She held out a short stack of messages for my spindle, giving that unmistakably all-knowing grin of hers. "And about that hatchet job you posted overnight? You're not trying for Mr. Popularity any place, are you?"

I gave her a look to let her know nothing was going to spoil my mood today. She just pointed at the door to the stairway leading to our editor-in-chief.

"Up you go, young man. Mm Hmm!" I nodded a 'thanks' for the messages as I added them to my overgrown collection. I recognized an unanswered invitation envelope about midway down the spindle, but headed upstairs.

When Larry Galica first opened this storefront news service inside of a hundred year old wooden balloon frame commercial building, he had the side entrance nailed shut and a doorway cut out from inside the office itself as the access to the second floor staircase, where he had taken up residence from day one. He had been a reporter with a number of neighborhood newspapers from the 1980's forward, and had seen most of them close their doors as markets changed or moved or dried up. The once mighty newspaper industry found its match in television and instant 24-hour news broadcasts. The news didn't get any better, just more plentiful, Larry often enjoyed saying.

Chicago has been home to some of the greatest newspapers and news dynasties this country has ever produced. Both citywide and local newspapers have thrived across the entire history of 'the city of big shoulders'. The Chicago Daily News, the Herald, the Sun, the Times, Zgoda, Chicago Tribune, Chicago Today, the Sun-Times, the American, the World (a socialist daily), the Daily Calumet and others produced some brilliant writers and reporters across their existence, including Henry Justin Smith, Mike Royko, Ben Hecht, Charles Macarthur, Carl Sandburg (Google him some time!) and a guy named Robert Hardy Andrews. One of my favorites, Andrews would go on to create and write for radio programs such as "Jack Armstrong the All-American Boy" and "Ma Perkins". He also wrote short stories that became classic Hollywood films, like "If I Had A Million." I'm not entirely sure what Chicago's newspapers are producing in their reporters today.

Larry Galica and I had first met the day of the fire, the aftermath anyway, nearly twenty years ago. Twenty years. He interviewed me off the back end of an ambulance on Houston Avenue, where the techs had checked me out and were giving oxygen to two of the kids, and me. Concise questions, but with a sincerity behind them. He cared. About me, the kids, the neighborhood. Without trying not to, I never did tell him, or anyone, why I was there that day. A white boy in the 'jungle' as a lot of cops and reporters would call the 'hood, off the record. With a handgun under the front seat of my Nova.

On the wall along the stairway to his office were front-page printouts of some of the Service's success stories, mixed in with images from around the neighborhood. A couple of the articles up there were by yours truly. I knocked on the door at the top of the stairs.

"C'mon in, Nicky!" A voice called. I opened the door.

The apartment upstairs had been converted into a small hospital ward, for one patient. The white painted walls were very bright with the morning sunlight pouring in from the southern windows. Larry was in his hospital bed, in an upright position, with pillows holding him up from the back. With some medical monitors alongside the bed, he had a rolling overhang table supporting a large laptop and papers, which he slid aside when I walked in. With everything else going on with him, Larry still wore a clean white short-sleeved shirt and tie during summer business hours. Hair finger-combed but in place, what was left of it. He was a lot thinner now than when I started this job.

"I'd like your copy early today, if you can do it. A couple of the nationals picked up your killer blog overnight and are already calling for follow ups, Nicky. You can thank me later for the editing."

"How'd it turn out?"

"Don't you read your own blog?"

"Not if I can help it. I read them when I write them, I guess."

"There's a copy of the finished work in my printer. Help yourself, Nicky."

I stepped around Larry's bed to his printer off to one side, pulling out the one-page blog. Elements were familiar but Larry had done quite a number on it:

"This morning I woke up to the news that the world had become a much better place to live and breathe, because Joey Miller is dead.

"Joseph A. Miller started out as a two-bit hustler. He was a common thief who worked his way into the trust of local community organizations, and eventually into the office of the Alderman of the 10th Ward, where it was widely rumored he served as a bag and button man for the suburban syndicate and an all around thug for an unwitting community organizer who would go on to become Alderman Anthony Coronado.

"Joey Miller was an official suspect in at least three separate unsolved homicides. He was also arrested but never convicted on several counts of assault and extortion. In most cases, key witnesses developed amnesia or simply disappeared before he could be indicted. In other cases, the indictments are still sitting on the desks of our elected prosecutors, waiting for some incorruptible soul to serve them in some unbuyable court. Well, thanks guys, I guess the wait is over.

"Joey stank of the graft and corruption he made happen out of his union hall office down on Burnham Avenue all those years after he muscled his way into the door. And the stench rubbed off on anyone who worked with him, from the alderman on down the line. A tough guy who city workers and politicians could always hit up for a donation or a pledge or a favor, never asking what scummy pocket he had to pick to hand all that sweaty cash over to whatever problem du jour had their attention for the moment.

"There will undoubtedly be an emperor's funeral for the late great Joseph Miller, because in this town we always seem to hail and worship the worst among us. From Capone to Blagojevich, it's in the nature of Chicago itself. For the law abiding citizens of Chicago, it's a time to celebrate!"

"Thanks for keeping the mood intact, boss! I wasn't really sure you were going to post any of it. I'll have tonight's blog up before I leave the office."

"That'll be fine, Nicky. As for last night's blog, I like avoiding lawsuits whenever I'm able, but you should expect some blowback from Miller's fans."

"You want more on pal Joey, I suppose?" Larry enjoyed it whenever I could tie in an old movie to any present situation.

"He's who's selling today, my friend, and you helped make that happen." Looking up from the spare paperwork in his lap Larry noticed the reluctance on my face, I guess. "Unless you had something else in mind?"

"What I'd like to write is a piece about Leon Perez, the guy who was murdered yesterday morning in my building on 95th? I knew him for some time. He was in that book. You know which one I mean?"

"Yeah, I'm in that book, too. There's a copy in the library downstairs if you need it. Should be anyway, if another writer didn't make off with it. Can you recall what man of the hour wasn't in that book, Nicky?"

I nodded, and smiled a bit. I thought I could get away from the Joey story for at least a day, but no such luck. Larry offered a solution for both of our problems.

"How about real bios this time, about each of them, show the similarities and contrasts, let the reader know how each one mattered to you, and the neighborhood, as far as you feel comfortable with." Larry got me. "If you can give me something from Joey's angle then I'll cover his alleged suburban syndicate contacts. I've got some favors to call in from the State's Attorney's office, anyhow. That'll sell some ad space!"

"Yeah, I think I could do that. I'm gonna need a little time for some research at Bowen today."

"You got plenty of it. Post by 5 pm. Okay, Nicky?" After a little laugh Larry's attention went back to the papers on his table. His nurse walked in from the kitchen area and I headed out.

Larry was one of the best reporters remaining in South Chicago who never did get out of the neighborhood when bigger opportunities had knocked. Born and reared in Harvey, a small suburb south of Chicago, he was another lifer. Having never married, he lived with his mom until well after his dad died, and for a while longer after Larry himself was diagnosed with a motor neuron disease, similar to amyotrophic lateral sclerosis, ALS, caused by the polio virus. He too had been a model railroad buff before his situation limited his mobility in getting to his basement pike. Larry specialized in the Rock

Island line, in HO scale. I remember seeing photos of his layout in the basement of his home in Harvey in old copies of the Daily Calumet.

———————

Antonio Coronado was not looking forward to the next few minutes and had tried to pass off the responsibility to his executive secretary, to no avail. Despite his long haul in local politics and more than a bit of a chip on his shoulder, he really was not a confrontational man. It helped having muscle on staff for any real battles. Chances are he lost the will to fight as a boy with his mother's help, or better yet, from witnessing her affect on his father across the years. At least Tony had gotten a heads up from Vic Hanley as to their arrival.

Passing through his inner office to the front entrance, Coronado greeted the detectives and led them into his private office closing the door behind them.

"Please." He indicated the padded chairs in front of his desk for their use. "How may I be of service, gentlemen?"

"Alderman Coronado, as a courtesy to your office we would like to ask you a few questions about the whereabouts of two of your office employees on the night of Tuesday past," stated detective Arden Sasuta, nearing retirement and looking like it.

"Which two would that be?"

Flipping open a notepad, Sasuta named Eduardo Z and Bernard P. Detective Gabriel Ramirez, Sasuta's youthful Latino partner, silently confirmed the two names on his iPad.

Coronado nodded. "They worked directly under the late Joseph Miller, who, well I don't know their day to day activities of course." Antonio got up from his desk. "They should be in their office next door right now if - "

"There'll be time for that, Alderman." Antonio sat back down. "Insofar as you're concerned, however, they did not answer directly to you?" Sasuta asked.

"No. Joseph, Joey, brought them in when he was hired by this office about seven years ago, I believe."

"Of course you weren't the alderman at that time, Alderman," Sasuta pointed out.

Coronado wondered what notes Sasuta's partner, Detective Ramirez, was taking. "Pardon? No, at that time I was a community activist and we were building a fine political organization for the improvement of the community. Do either of you live in the community, detectives?"

"No sir, I'm originally from Roseland," responded Detective Sasuta. Ramirez just shook his head.

"Well, we're on the way back! With the upcoming change in developers at the Lakeside –"

Sasuta cut him off. "Yes Alderman, since hiring your two employees, are you aware of any activities outside this office they may have been involved in that might give you pause as to their continued employment in this office?"

Coronado could only think of about a dozen. "No. No! Of course not! I barely interact with them, or have, not, since they came on board. Really, Joey was their supervisor, in their work, for this office. I'm not aware of their after-work activities, or if they even have any."

"Are they considered precinct captains in your ward organization, Alderman Coronado?" Both Antonio and Sasuta were surprised when Detective Ramirez spoke up.

"No. Eduardo and Bernard are not directly involved as precinct captains, Detective," said Coronado.

"Then, what do they do here for you and the ward, Alderman?" Ramirez asked.

Sasuta cut in before Coronado could answer. "Well it's only a matter of routine that we have to ask these questions, Alderman. You know the mayor is keeping an eye on this case, closely." Coronado nodded approvingly. He had not known how closely the mayor was watching this case, but now he did. Sasuta got up, followed by Ramirez, still taking notes on his iPad. "We'll drop in next door and interview your two employees now."

Coronado rose and escorted the detectives through the outer hall and up to the office door of the meeting room, the place looking more like a floral shop. He opened the door for them but did not enter the space.

Walking slowly back to his office, Coronado wondered why they hadn't asked him where he was the night Joey got what he deserved. Or about the money Joey had with him. He walked back into his office, giving a shrug to Lynn as he passed her doorway. She thought he looked a couple of shades lighter than usual. He closed his office door. Lynn noticed the light on Tony's private line light up.

Several minutes later, Coronado exited his office and walked into Lynn's, closing the door behind him. Carrying a hand-written note, he handed it to Lynn, with an index finger on his lips to indicate silence. Lynn read the note, nodded and walked with him out of her office and out into the main entrance hall, down the stairs and out the building. Once they had turned into the alleyway separating the Fink building from a drug store parking lot, he spoke, still wary of anyone around them.

"I want you to use an outside line to call the number on the paper and arrange for the sweep, right away. Today if they can," he said a bit nervously.

"Do you really think it's possible?" Lynn wondered.

"I just got off the phone with my cousin Fred, from Homeland Security. I thought he might know why the feds were sniffing around and he asked me point blank if the FBI had removed the bugs from Joey's office yet! I asked Fred, what were they bugging him for? He said he didn't know, but I'd better watch my own ass! Have the contractor start with the offices next door, and do a sweep of our space, too, just in case. I'll arrange something for those two thugs to do to get them out of the office when the time comes."

"First the murder and now the offices are bugged? It's starting to get too scary, Tony. None of us signed up for this, including you and my sister. You need to pass all this by your attorney."

"Yeah, I know. Go now and arrange it, okay?" He looked around as someone who looked familiar walk past at a distance, just realizing he was outside the office without his suit coat on. "Make it after hours so the staff will have cleared out." He watched as Lynn walked over to the bank building across the street to use a payphone, one of the few left on Commercial Avenue.

Though the summer session had ended the week before, I figured somebody would still be working at Bowen High School, either getting set for the fall or cleaning up from the summer. I pulled to a stop in front of the main entrance, parking on the Bessemer Park side of East 89th Street. I still get a chill of regret whenever I go back to my old high school. How about you?

Checking my watch, I knew I'd have to hustle if I wanted to be on time for my docent work at the museum. I wasn't quite sure what I was looking for here or where my next story would lead. Inspiration comes from strange places.

The front doors were wide open as there was a white five-ton box truck parked on the wide sidewalk with its back end towards the entrance. I had forgotten that the Mendoza mural was being moved today. Another reporter for the Service, Felicia Gonzalez, was covering the story.

There she was at the doorway, mid-20's, a full head shorter than me, a striking beauty with dark, almost black hair flowing past her shoulders, wearing a dress a little too high above her knees and a little too low cut up top for the comfort of roving eyes.

"Hello there!" I said with a smile.

"Hi, Nick. Did you come to watch?"

"No, just doing some research. How's the move going?"

"Slow! And I mean slow! That mural does not want to leave the building. I can't understand why - I was glad to get out!" Here was yet another victim of the Chicago Public Schools system.

"Yeah, but look how far we got!" We shared a laugh as I walked into the massive structure and felt the sudden 10-degree drop in temperature. These old buildings, put up before air conditioning was the norm, had their own methods of keeping the inmates cool.

James Harvey Bowen, for whom the school is named, was a Republican state boss and first president of the Calumet & Chicago Canal & Dock Company. Through that instrument, Bowen and his associates helped bring about the construction of piers, docks, bridges and other public improvements to the area, more than 145 years back.

Bowen was also instrumental in convincing major industrial giants to build their steel plants on the lakefront, effectively closing off access to the lakeshore for use by the residents, from 79th Street to just south of the mouth of the Calumet River. Of course back then swimming was not the usual activity of the working class. The development of Calumet Park directly to the south of these steel plants came much later in the history of South Chicago.

I took a left in the hallway and headed straight to the main office. Somehow the grandness of the hallway had faded as years passed, it just seemed a lot smaller to me. A young Black student, most likely an incoming sophomore on summer work detail, was holding the office door open. Apple green earplugs were inserted into his ears, the cables tracing down into his low-hanging, baggy pants pocket. At least he had on-the-job entertainment.

Stepping into the bright office, I could see the principal's private domain just ahead. A bevy of busy workers, mostly in white t-shirts and khakis, college-age, were shifting another piece of the puzzle off the far wall of the office. The mural must have been painted in the mid to late 1970's, and was behind a curtain by the time I attended Bowen. Our principal then didn't care much for the artwork, I guess. Painted by the brothers Mendoza, Victor and Francisco, the mural was now on its way to a new home and hopefully more notoriety in the modern wing of the Art Institute downtown.

This move made economic sense even if it was just more local art treasure leaving the 'hood. With the Board of Education in an eternal state of fiscal mess and with little chance that the taxing bodies of the city, county or state would come to the aid of inner city children any time soon, the B of E took the last poison pill they could find. By selling off their internal artworks, murals, statuary and rare books getting dusty on library shelves, they had raised enough cash to avoid another strike by the teachers union. At least for the next year. Five million for this one piece of art was a steal.

Francisco Mendoza was a recurring subject in that book from the library I had to study on site. At the time, he had completed a neighborhood mural for the South Chicago YMCA. Known as the 'Boxer Mural', it was painted on three walls and the ceiling in the little gym of the 'Y', an iconic neighborhood institution that somehow survived the mills' extinction. Years later, after Francisco had left

South Chicago only to flourish as an art teacher in Pilsen where his art was appreciated and later coveted, the Boxer Mural was destroyed to make way for an expanded day care program at the YMCA.

I stepped out of the offices just as another slab of wall was precariously rolled out diagonally through the doorway. The young monitor didn't flinch. Must be some good tunes coming out of those earplugs.

Like most of the students who had passed through these halls since the place opened, outside of the yearbooks, there probably wasn't a trace of Leon Perez left at Bowen. At least the tributes to veterans of several generations who once attended the school had been maintained over the years, displayed on the walls along the hallways. I'd have to refer to my notes for some quotes I had from Leon, for the blog.

Walking around the place, you'd think I'd get some inspiration, but nothing yet. I opened one in a row of wooden doors to the auditorium, which in my mind had somehow always looked much larger from the outside, with its green domed roof. Inside, I wondered how much longer the two murals flanking the stage could afford to remain for the current and future students to enjoy. There were a few students acting out on the stage, a mix of dance and drama with a boy at the piano, reaching for Earl Hynes, but coming up a little short. No worries. Good to see younger people still had some faith in their dreams.

It was often an interesting side note to me, that James Bowen hadn't lived to see the rise of South Chicago after all his efforts. Though he never actually lived in the neighborhood, Colonel Bowen maintained an estate at the south end of Roseland, west of Pullman, along the banks of the Grand Calumet. He also had a mansion on Michigan Avenue in the heart of the city, which had been destroyed in the great Chicago fire of 1871.

On May 1st, 1881, Bowen was riding in a horse-drawn carriage along South Chicago Avenue when a steam train engine blew its whistle, causing the horse to rear up and jostle the carriage. At that time the train tracks, which are now above the street traffic, were at street level. Bowen was thrown out and onto the roadway, causing a mortal wound. He was carried a few steps to the South Chicago Hotel, where he died of his injuries.

Stepping back into the hallways, I wandered the place for a time, passing rows of glass cases filled with trophies, plaques and photographs of past sports teams and then, there it was. An altar, no, a shrine to the late, great Joey Miller himself. 'What? No bronze bust?' I thought. Maybe a victory wreath crowning his head like Cicero would have been too much, even for Bowen. Someone had recently added black and purple bunting to the large stand-alone case.

Hanging on the back wall of that special case, a framed team photograph, blown up so you could make out the faces of all the other players and the coaches from that magical first season of Joey Miller at Bowen High. Nobody was smiling but you'd figure that the photographer must have told the team to 'Look tough!' No, that wasn't it, I knew that. Everybody looked as miserable as they really felt that inglorious day. I finally found the face of the kid I was looking for. I did look a lot thinner back then.

Yeah, in case you haven't guessed it by now, that was my jockstrap Joey shoved his fist down into in the Eckersall Stadium locker room, when we were both freshmen players, more than a half a life ago. I'm not in any of the other team photos with the late Joey Miller because I only played football in my freshman year. Instead, I went out for the track team, concentrated on writing and history classes.

Looking for another face on that photo, I found, what was his name? Paul Zitnik, maybe? I probably haven't thought about him since high school. Like me, Paul didn't move on to sophomore football at Bowen, either. That summer after freshman year, he committed suicide, but the school didn't really talk about it much that fall and, like a lot of people from our past, he was forgotten. Looking at that picture, as I thought about Paul, a scrawny kid under all that padding on the field and the football squad and Joey's taunting and tormenting anything that appeared weak to him, it all came flowing back. Everything I didn't want to remember. Every dirty trick I witnessed or heard of from the time I met Joey Miller all the way to the present and what I discovered he was pulling on the grunt cops and organizations on the southeast side. I knew I had my story, and I wouldn't be holding anything back.

Since we're getting to know each other now, let me tell you that I met Anne Marie Benedetto when I was working in my senior year as a stock boy at Gately's Peoples Store, a big department store that covered half a block at 112th and Michigan Avenue, in Roseland. She was buying candy for her mother a few aisles over from where I was stocking men's hosiery, a more fancy name for socks.

Anne Marie was a year younger than I, attending St. Francis de Sales High School on the East Side, but we saw a lot of each other for a couple of months before I graduated from Bowen. She went with me to my prom. I had my first used car back then, a 1972 four-door Chevy Nova, in an olive green color. The Nova had an engine too powerful for the body GM had placed it in. She was very lovely. Anne Marie, I mean.

We even had a couple of picnics on the lakefront in Cal Park, after my graduation, on my days off from stock work. Anne Marie made her own schedule at the restaurant. I remember how embarrassed she was by her family's reaction to me when I was first introduced to them, not being of Italian descent and all. I guess some people are still like that now. After that we more or less drifted apart, though we did exchange Christmas cards and some small gifts that first holiday after we ended it.

Her funeral Mass was at St. Anthony's on 116th Street, a large red brick shrine with bright, gleaming white marble statuary adorning its altars. I don't know the details about how she and Joey first hooked up, but I know it was shortly after she had graduated high school, and that he didn't bother to attend her very crowded, very sad funeral. I was hunting for Joey Miller on Houston Avenue, a couple of days after Ann Marie's funeral, when I saw those kids screaming from the second floor of that burning house, which kind of changed everything.

———

Just inside the Office of the Mayor on the fifth floor of City Hall is a wood paneled foyer with portraits and photographs of all of the past mayors of our great city. It's a fine place to cool your heels while waiting for an audience with the current occupant of that office. Lieutenant Vic Hanley sat on a padded bench off to one side and out of view of the bustling exterior hallway, with hat in hand, tapping a CD jewel box, patiently awaiting his private weekly briefing with the mayor.

"He'll see you now, Lieutenant," an executive secretary said. He stood and straightened his uniform coat, and was ushered into the inner sanctum. Not for the first time, my friend Vic Hanley was playing both sides of the fence. Welcome to Chicago politics!

Cruising the 'hood in their black '66 Pontiac GTO, Eduardo Z and Bernard B tried to get a handle on themselves after the grilling by Detectives Sasuta and Ramirez on their own turf. They ended up at the Eugene Flag Company on 79th Street near Stony Island. Bernard had caused a bit of a row when he made his usual u-turn across four lanes of traffic to park in front of the store, but when he opened his wallet for the officer who had immediately pulled up alongside, and flashed his St. Joseph's patch next to his driver's license, all was well. It's good to know somebody in a town like Chicago.

Their high school pal and sometime ward 'activist', Dwayne W, had worked his way up from a stock boy at Eugene Flag to the head of the shipping department, of which he was the lone member, since he had dropped out of senior year at Bowen to pursue a career in petty crime. Eduardo Z and Bernard P had an extracurricular task in mind for their convenient friend, who fenced scorched and warmed over items on the side, among other activities known and unknown to the police. In Chicago everybody has to have at least two jobs to survive.

"S'up, clowns?" greeted Dwayne when he spotted his oft-time compatriots winding their way around tables and bales of finished, though unpacked flags and banners.

"Dwayne, my man!" shouted Eduardo over the vibrating sounds of multiple sewing machines. A number of Latinas of various ages sat at those machines in the back room of the narrow facility, completing more flags of all sizes. Somewhere a radio played Mexican dance tunes, similar in tempo to polkas, but with Spanish lyrics.

"Whatchu doin' outta yo' comfort zone?" Dwayne asked while trading man hugs with the boys.

"Damn man, ain't you heard 'bout our Joey, man?" Bernard asked, with genuine surprise.

"Numbah one story 'round here, my brothas!" Dwayne acknowledged, pointing to his heart. "Breaks my heart to see him go like dat. Know what I'm sayin'?"

"He was da man!" Eduardo agreed.

"Da man," Bernard echoed.

"But now we got ourselves a problem, Dwayne," Eduardo began. "See? It's like this. Wit'out our Joey, we got no muscle. Our cops ain't callin' in, couple a the old boys up and called it quits on us, man. Fuckin' precinct captains that we made!"

"It's like we stopped and the world kept turning without us, man!" Bernard added his frustration.

"I hear ya, my brothas. But word on the street is you's in da shits," Dwayne pointed out. "That whole 10th Ward organ-I-ZAY-shun is gone wit' da wind. Like a vacuum, it done got sucked up! City's on da warpath!"

"Yeah, well, they're only gonna bury one of us come Saturday, man!" Eduardo was getting worked up.

"Just sayin' like it is, Lalo, jus' lettin' you's two know it ain't no bizniz as *uswalmente no mas, mi hermanos*! You gotta lay low!" Looking around as if sensing danger, Dwayne tried to let the boys know how it was. "Yo alderman done fucked the works, not Joey. Buttin' heads wit' da mayor? Sheet!"

"What've I been sayin', Cuz?" Eduardo told Bernard. "Manza fuckin' train wreck!"

"You don't wanna be 'round when da shit comes down on dat mofo, no how! But no sweat, my brothas! You's just gotta lay low and let what's comin' come on down!"

"C'mon down!" Bernard agreed. "Like on the Price Is Right!"

"Yeah, wit' all respects to the dead, man, once our Joey's six feet under we'll lay low, we'll lay low, Dwayne." Eduardo reasoned with himself. The three exchanged man hugs around again.

"So whatchu got fo' me, my brothas?" Dwayne kept it all business, rubbing his large hands together.

"C'mon out to our ride and check it out! Know anything about bells, Dwayne?" Bernard asked.

Usually I didn't borrow equipment from the office, but today was going to be tight, and I was glad to have that laptop with me as I walked into the Calumet Park field house just before one p.m. A group of people was already waiting for the museum to open, including some downtown reporters. After yesterday's news coverage, this kind of public notoricty could be expected. I could see past the doorway gates that there was already activity in the museum hall, catching a glimpse of the two detectives assigned to Leon's case.

I made my way through the small crowd towards the gated entry. Barney Janecki, president of the historical society, warmly greeted me and let me inside.

"Thanks, Barney! Quite a crowd today!"

"Not a surprise, though the police coming in early was a good one on us," Barney replied. "Surprise, that is. You bring some homework with you?" he asked, spotting the laptop under my arm.

"I'm a little behind in my Service work, today," I let him know.

"Well, you just find some room on the research side and get comfortable. I'm gonna open up in a minute or two."

"Thanks, Barney. Let me just get settled in. I'm here to work the door, too!"

"I want to talk to you about your article from yesterday, Nick, if we get some time today." He was a little firm about it.

"Sure. No problem, Barney."

Glancing over to the broken case wall to the right, where the detectives and a uniformed officer, probably a tech, had gathered, I made a beeline behind the file shelving on my left to a more private domain in the one-room museum. A patch of wall where the bell had been was being dusted for prints. I thought Detective Ducree might have spotted me when I had entered. Gloria Novak, the society's corresponding secretary, was already seated at the round table near the room's large picture windows, reading through incoming mail for the society.

"Afternoon, Gloria," I greeted her. "How are you doing today?"

Looking up from her paperwork, "Hey Nicky! I read your piece in the Calumet. Really, Nicky?"

I could see this might not be the best place to settle in. "Gotta write 'em as I see them, Gloria. There's a lot of stuff I haven't put in yet that helps make my point." I was almost apologetic without having any reason to be. "You didn't know him like I did." I kept moving farther towards the back wall. Gloria wasn't convinced.

"He's not even buried yet, Nicky. What do you imagine his family thinks about an article like that?"

"Chances are they never really knew the guy." I was almost safely out of sight.

"Well it's a shame." Gloria went back to her papers but I couldn't remember her looking more upset about anything.

Finding a partially vacant shelf to set the laptop on, I opened it up and started in on what turned out to be a lengthy, more personal and professional follow-up to last night's diatribe in blog form.

———

His office wasn't the biggest space in the place, especially if more than one person needed to pace the floor at the time, but with the meeting hall filled to the rim with floral presentations, it would have to do. Lynn ushered Alderman Davis of the 8th Ward and Alderman Brevert of the 7th Ward into Antonio Coronado's private domain, such as it was.

"Welcome! Welcome, friends!" Antonio greeted his council compatriots sincerely. "Everybody take a seat. Anybody need a drink? Coffee? Water?"

"Got anything stronger?" asked Alderman Todd Brevert. About the same age as Antonio, also a first-term alderman, but with a different route to an alderman's desk through poverty as a young Black boy in South Shore. Brevert was also on the outs with the mayor, naturally.

"Sorry Todd, I don't keep any liquor in the place. That'll be all for now, Lynn, thank you."

"Love what you've done with the place, Tony," Alderman Marion Davis of the 8th Ward said, looking around. "Where did you get all the historic photos?" She reached into her large purse beside her chair on the floor and pulled out a fifth of some light brown liquid, offering it to Alderman Brevert. He accepted the bottle and helped himself to a plastic cup off of a side table, pouring himself more than a shot.

"They came with the place," Antonio said offhandedly. His staff saw to such menial things as office décor. "Anybody hear from Charlie today?" Brevert shook his head 'No.'

"I have not and I don't expect to and neither should either of you," Alderman Davis responded. "He hasn't returned my calls since last night. I'm wondering if the long hand of the fifth floor hasn't reached out to our esteemed associate?"

Alderman Marion Davis was an apprentice of the late Stroger machine in the 8th Ward, a confident, middle-aged Black woman with the political sense to know when to strike for gold and when to call it a day. Today was not the latter day. Tied to this cabal, she was finally getting noticed by the right people in the right circles.

"Charlie's been around long enough to know what side his bread is buttered on. Remember what Daley did to your Buchanan after the '95 election? He shut him down out here, Tony!" said Alderman Brevert, after finishing off his drink. "That kind of clout is still only a phone call away."

Alderman Todd Brevert was another mayoral appointee biting the hand of his political master in this secession move. A perennial candidate in the 7th Ward, across more than a decade Brevert had run, and lost, every race for every seat on the ballot, before finally obtaining the alderman's post. Mayors often pick and choose the appointees most likely to blow up in their faces, or so it would seem.

"We all got a lesson from old man Buchanan," Alderman Davis concurred. "You should see the photo I have in my office of your Buchanan, Tony, and my John Stroger at some ground-breaking thing out here in the Tenth, lookin' like two old war horses!" she said fondly.

"I knew he'd be the first to cave," Coronado mused. "And our mayor doesn't carry that kind of clout around in his pockets anymore, Marion. Not since those police execution tapes went public. I'd be surprised if he even bothers to run in the next election."

"Is that what this is all about, Tony? A mayoral bid?" inquired Alderman Brevert, smiling a short grin.

"After that land grab deal with the mega church in Charlie's 9th Ward, I was surprised he even got reelected. And he's got no place to go. Politically, who'd want to run an old man?" Marion bluntly stated. "On the other hand, the mayor will always be the mayor, in this town anyway, as long as he wants the seat."

"Yeah, the mayor's been smelling blood on the waters in the 9th for some time," Brevert agreed. He helped himself to another drink.

"So it comes down to we three, my friends," Antonio concluded.

"The Cook County elections board wants to slate me in the fall for a state senate seat, so I'll expect both of ya'lls support and help in the campaign," Alderman Davis said. "I was kinda hoping for a generous donation from the late Mr. Miller, but now?" She shrugged. "And don't be too hard on ol' Charlie, Tony. He's a survivor, which is somethin' we all have to learn how to do, or drown in this town."

"Don't worry about my support, I don't forget my friends, Marion. I don't forget my enemies, either," Antonio forewarned.

"That's good policy if you're being serious about this mayoral bid thang," she countered. "You are being serious about it, aren't you, Tony?"

There was a knock on the door. Lynn stuck her head inside. "Alderman Coronado? Alderman Crooks is here for your meeting." She ushered Alderman Charles Crooks into the office. The three original aldermen looked at each other in various degrees of surprise.

"Welcome, Charlie! Welcome!" Antonio stepped over to the doorway to greet and help his friend find a seat. Alderman Crooks walked with the aid of a finely carved wooden cane with a sterling silver handle, which made his movements slow and deliberate.

"Here, Charlie! Come sit by me!" invited a perked up Alderman Davis.

"Need a drink?" Alderman Brevert offered.

———————————

After pressing the 'send' button, filing my somewhat lengthy follow-up blog with the Service, I sat back for a moment, wondering about the blowback repercussions to come. All the unanswered questions my family, friends and colleagues had about me over a couple of decades were about to be starkly though honestly answered.

"Nick? You still back there? Someone's asking for you," Gloria called through the metal shelving, where I had snuck back to between docent duties at the doorway. Most of the volunteer work on open day consisted of greeting people at the door and inviting them to sign their names in the guest book. Not much actual work unless a researcher stopped in, but a good public relations turn for the Historical Society. Sometimes I got lucky and had a question or two posed by a visitor and then I could go on a hunting expedition through the archives. Most of the docents were familiar with the overall collection, but everybody had a specialty, whether in social organizations, labor movements or something as simple as the array of movie theatres the community boasted over the decades. Of course, none of them existed by the time I started attending movies as a boy with my parents. Few of the buildings that housed them still stood as a testament to the times. My specialty? I knew all about railroads.

I checked my watch. A quarter to three! Made the deadline with hours to spare. I stepped out from behind the stacks.

"Good afternoon, Mr. Daniels." It was Detective Ducree, looking as unfazed by life today as she did in that interrogation room yesterday. "We're finished with our investigation here and I wanted to say 'goodbye' and thank you for last night." Gloria gave me a look and stepped ever too slowly away from the conversation. I did not need this.

"You sure can turn a phrase, Detective." Those eyes of hers again.

"I'm just sorry I have to go now. We didn't get a chance to chat."

"Maybe next time we run into each other, Detective."

"Count on it, Mr. Daniels." She did that smile thing again like last night at headquarters and turned, walking towards the exit. I watched her go, until I saw the look Gloria was giving me. I got back to my shelf space and packed up my gear. At least I didn't have to deal with Ducree's partner, Detective Ex-boxer.

"Nick, we didn't get time to talk about your article," Gloria pointed out as I made my own way towards the exit outta there.

"Gloria, I promise, all of your questions and doubts should be more than answered with tonight's blog!" Anyway, even if they weren't, I wouldn't step inside the museum for nearly another week.

"Well I should hope so!"

I made it up to the checkout desk, a remnant of the long-ago library that once occupied this room, where Barney was standing, talking with some guests. I nodded and waved my thanks as I passed by, the gated exit door in sight! I almost made it.

Standing directly in the doorway was a man I looked up to. Literally. About a half-head taller than me, Joe Mulac was a walking neighborhood institution. Another retiree from the steel industry, but from the management side of the business, in his retirement Joe rekindled his love of drawing and painting, producing hundreds of watercolor drawings of the important edifices of the community. His artworks were now hanging in bank lobbies, offices, museums and better households. There was a watercolor of the Calumet Park field house hanging in my living room.

"Nick! Leaving early? Just the man I was looking for!" Joe said in that booming voice of his that made heads turn. He clamped a hand on my shoulder. Now I was going to get it. "I have to talk to you about that article of yours last night!"

Caught at last, I surrendered. "Yes, Joe?" He moved his face close to mine.

Almost whispering, "Nicky, I just wanted to thank you for having the balls to tell the truth about that guy. Somebody had to pull their head out of the sand and I'm glad it was you." My mouth was open but nothing was coming out.

Finally I uttered, "Thanks a lot, Joe. I really appreciate that." He smiled and patted my shoulder, letting me pass through the door as he made his way into the museum. What I needed was a walk around the park, and a chocolate milkshake from Skyway Dog House wouldn't hurt, either. Did I have lunch today?

Arriving back at the office a little after five, I found Louise had left for the day, right on her own schedule, but a preprinted sign was attached to the front back of my chair. All it said was 'Upstairs'. Another reporter was interviewing someone with his back towards me in one of the side offices. I gave a wave to the reporter and headed upstairs.

"I read your copy. Are you sure you want all that out there, Nick?" asked my bedridden editor.

"Everything I'm comfortable with. That's what you said this morning, boss!" I could kid around like that with Larry, but he knew I was too serious to be talked out of this. At least I hoped that clearly came across in my filed blog.

"I really didn't know most of this background on you and Joey Miller." Larry paused a moment, a question was coming. "I never even thought to ask you why you were on Houston that day Nick, with the kids and the fire. Damn! Where were you Tuesday night, anyway?"

Smiling, I said, "The police have already double-checked my alibi, if that becomes an issue. And I don't think there's a law out there that could convict me for unattempted murder. Is that even a word, 'unattempted'?"

"Not this week but give social media some time, it'll make Webster's in a year or two. You got a flack jacket in that Lincoln of yours?" We laughed a little nervously together. "He had a lot of friends who aren't going to like this follow-up to yesterday's blog one bit."

"A lot of it's ancient history. Nearly twenty years. Anyway, you're my editor, Larry. You get the final cut on this. As always."

"No way, Nick." He tapped his laptop. "This may be the best thing you've written for the Service. Certainly it's the most personal. I'll have to pass this one by the lawyers, but I'll stand with your story just as you wrote it, once you really finish it. My worries are in the potential repercussions of telling the truth to a city not used to reading it, not comfortable with knowing it. Also, I don't think we should limit this for your overnight, I think it's something for the weekly, on line and in print."

I didn't expect that, but every writer and reporter hopes for a spot at the top. Wait a minute. "Once I finish it?"

Larry handed me a piece of paper. "You may want to include this. Preliminary DNA findings on an unborn baby boy that died in a bus crash about twenty years ago. I guess the system never had Joey's blood at their disposal before yesterday. Good to know they can keep evidence intact across decades when they want to."

I couldn't believe I was holding the missing link to Anne Marie and Joey Miller. I leaned against Larry's bedrail, my next words struggling to come out. "How did you get this?"

Larry was smiling. "Nice having friends out there, isn't it!"

I took a moment to compose myself and get back on track. "Should I clean the article up a bit for the gentry?" Larry had done extensive research and polling and came to the conclusion years ago that the print-reading customer was more sophisticated and sensitive than the daily blog subscribers we had reading our work. They expected, and got, more than just opinions. They also got a lot of coupons in their weekly, which has always been a big draw.

"If I were you, I wouldn't change a word beyond your additions. As your editor, I'm not going to. As your friend, and you know, Nick, I am your friend, I hope you're ready to duck once this is in print!" We both had another laugh, which he didn't do often enough. "The contrast you play between Miller and your friend Leon, rich man poor man, is brilliant! You've got back-up for all this?" I nodded. "Got any ideas what you're going to put in it's place for tonight's blog?"

"Probably something simple, like tolerance of the truth in the twenty-first century!" I smiled and got out of there before Larry changed his mind, which I knew he wouldn't.

I did have plans for the evening, but they would have to sit on a sidetrack 'til I got a make-up story on line. I had mixed feelings about my copy making the weekly paper, but I was both relieved for the extra time before it came to print and nervous about what I had to tell a few people about what was in the article. I didn't want to let them read it first, before hearing about it from me. That was a writer's responsibility, and I had to talk to them in the next thirty-six hours.

After I filed my article and left the Service offices, Larry called in a favor from an old friend. He still had those out there, old friends with favors due, even from that hospital bed of his.

On Thursdays during the summer I had a standing invitation at Polish Jay's for a 'train run' with Jay and his young godsons and family, and I got to pick dinner for my train crew, which had to be from New Chop Suey. A fixture in South Chicago since 1984, it was the best Chinese food in the neighborhood. Being the only Chinese restaurant in the 'hood didn't hurt, but the food was by far the best south of Chinatown. I was a new staff writer/reporter for the Service when Pow Tsetung and his wife had moved to their current location on Commercial Avenue, with a grand opening that included dancing dragons, Chinese drummers and fireworks right on the sidewalk! It was a spectacle!

Entering the glass-front establishment, I made my way to the back of the restaurant, passing a few couples and groups of friends at the tables flanking both walls, enjoying their dinners, and each other's company. The space was clean but sparse, with Chinese inspired artwork decorating the walls.

There was a stocky Black man ordering take-out at the window ahead of me. He was having some trouble convincing the young cook behind the counter that the Cubs were a better baseball team than the White Sox. Each man was wearing an appropriate baseball cap in support of his preferred team. The eternal argument was interfering with the picking up of my dinner.

"Did you even see their stats last year? Well, didja?" the customer asked.

"Just tell me which team won the last World Series in this town! Name the team I give you free egg roll!" argued the young clerk.

"Do I get a free egg roll if I name the team?" I had to butt in. The Black man, who I recognized as one of the furniture movers from Steel City Furniture, gave me a look like I'd insulted his mother.

"Nick! Your order sitting here for half hour. I put in fresh egg rolls for you!" The clerk acknowledged me and got to it.

"Does Steel City know you're running around with advertising caps like that?" I said, smiling and pointing to the man's chappo.

Clutching his food close to his chest, the customer shared a laugh. "Yeah, the guy from the Calumet, alright! What they don't know won't hurt 'em, right?" And he headed for the exit.

"Okay, Nick. You need sweet sauce?' asked the clerk, trading my cash for two large bags of fresh-cooked food.

"Plenty! I'm feeding a train crew tonight! And don't forget the soy sauce!"

"You need plates?"

"No, we got everything else, thanks!"

Finally, dinner! I headed for the door, but noticed the figure of a large man looking in the window and darting out of sight when I started walking from the counter. By the time I made it out the door, he was nowhere to be seen. Only a few people waiting at the bus stop on 91st Street. Maybe he ducked down the alley. I thought better of it and stepped over to the Lincoln. I didn't shake the chill down my spine until I crossed under the Skyway viaduct, southbound on Commercial.

Train night in America! Polish Jay knew how to throw a bash, even if it came once a week during the summer, like clockwork. His deck out back had cool jazz wafting in the breeze, with Chinese-inspired lanterns dancing from wires strung across the space. A couple guests were splashing each other in the hot tub at the far end of the yard, while at the near side of the koi pond, a grill and tables were set up which he could monitor from his perch on the short deck above.

Jay had designed the five shipping containers, each with a familiar 'K-Line' advertising on their short ends, into a simple form, two on top of three on the bottom. The blank space above the box closest in to the backyard, afforded a big overlook balcony, with a metal staircase along the long side. The two upstairs containers held one large room, Jay's bedroom, the shared wall having been cut away by Advantage Structures, a local concern in the shipping container repurposing business. Completing the usual interior furnishings, bureaus and cabinets, was a massive queen-sized bed, with four carved wooden posts. As each one looked like an oversized corkscrew, Jay often called this his 'big screw bed'.

Meanwhile, two of the downstairs containers held equal floor space as the two above, for his kitchen, dining and bath areas, again with the first common wall cut away. The third self-contained box that faced north and opened into the cobblestone driveway with three overhead rollaway doors, Jay used for storage. The whole thing cost him a third of what any local bungalow would have. Clever recycling. If you like that warm, Cor-Ten steel feeling. I'm still a brick and mortar man, myself, but this did make a lot of sense. And it looked pretty cool.

When Jay bought the property from Hagberg's, there was still a ten-ton dry ice machine attached to the back of the building, which he eventually had cut to pieces and sold for scrap. But, being Jay, he waited until the Chinese were buying up scrap metal again before he had it demolished. He replaced it with a greenhouse, with an ornate wooden double-doorway that opened directly into the main building.

And in the main building, a modest, fifty-foot wide by seventy-six foot long with a rounded, sixteen foot height at its peak roof, was Jay's private domain, containing all the treasures of a man who never really grew up.

Entering from those wooden double-doors between the greenhouse and the main room, the entire space was filled with the sound of trains. Toy trains. O gauge toy trains, the kind every boy wanted under his Christmas tree, at least according to Johnny Cash from those old Lionel commercials. The pike was off to the left and consumed a full quarter of the interior space, with a wall of kitchen cabinets, counters and appliances halting its growth.

Between the entrance, storage shelving and the train pike was an inviting sitting area, with a big-screen television and stereo system, all neatly assembled on a large oriental rug. Beyond the sitting area and to the side of yet another, larger kitchen was Jay's library. With rows and rows of books on shelves and in glass-door cabinets, you'd have to figure the guy probably read most of them. I've borrowed a few myself. Quite a collection of books on Chicago. Probably helped a lot with his winnings on that game show, too.

Lining one side of the train pike were lit display cabinets, holding Jay's collections of Tootsie toy cars, other trains that didn't get 'played with' on the pike (wrong gauge), and a large collection of items from Chicago's two World's Fairs. Jay's parents both attended the 1933 fair, 'A Century of Progress'. Hanging from the three trusses inside the space, and on all the brick and finished surfaces, Jay had placed artworks, posters and signs from the neighborhood and all over Chicago. His collection included a few Francisco Mendoza paintings, a huge advertising sign that used to hang outside Ellis Cleaners, and a South Chicago Bank sign, before the name was changed to something else.

In the center of the display cabinets was an upright piano, which the kids would enjoy banging on until their fathers got fed up with the noise. Sometimes Jay would play a tune while everybody else did his or her own thing. Around Christmas he would put up a heavily decorated artificial tree to one side of the piano, which he claimed was from his own childhood, and play seasonal tunes while everybody sang their heads off. Lynn experienced all of this for the first time last Christmas. With all the sights and sounds, she was overwhelmed. She was also stunning in the twinkling lights. That may have been the moment I knew I was in love with her.

Farther on in the building was Jay's workspace, with two large tables, shelving, a woodshop by the front truck entrance, and a special table where the boys could assemble model train kits, to use here or on their own train pikes at home.

My crew was already working the two large train yards on the pike, lining up their freight trains, the older boys acting as yard masters for their younger brothers, cousins and friends. Two of the boys were Jay's godsons. Their fathers joined in the fun, too, between flipping burgers and soaking in the hot tub with their mates. I was always welcome because some of the engines and rolling stock were mine!

Usually I also got stuck with the passenger train work, which nobody else wanted to do. It wasn't as involved or complicated as the freight lines and rolling stock were, but I had my niche. The Rock Island Zephyr, just like the actual train at the Museum of Science and Industry, was my favorite. One of the freight yards on the pike resembled the real Short Line yard south of 95th Street and east of the Calumet River, complete with a scale model engine house. This section was one of my ideas on this grand train pike. Young engineers, even engineers young at heart, can't operate train empires on an empty stomach, so, first came dinner for all.

The Chinese food boxes and condiments had been spread out on a serving table outside and everybody just helped themselves to the feast, which included shrimp in lobster sauce, egg fu yung, assorted rice and meat dishes and plenty of fresh egg rolls to go around. Some of the younger people sported bathing suits, while other guests were in shorts and t-shirts with our host, Jay in his 'traditional' Thursday night loud Hawaiian shirt.

"No food inside!" Jay reminded his godsons, to which they replied in unison, "That's nice!" mocking one of Jay's oft heard comments. Of course, the youngest of the boys always tried to sneak back in before everybody else was done eating. Spending time with all the kids made me think about what kind of a father I'd make, when the time came. It also made me wonder, what was I waiting for?

Because of all that great noise from the multiple trains, the acoustics of the old building and a quick dip in the hot tub, and since I was having too much fun with the kids, I missed a text from Vic Hanley by half an hour. 'Meet me at Steve's for a drink, if you bring your ID.' it read. Ever notice how people over fifty use correct spelling and capitalization in their texting? I made my goodbyes and headed out of Polish Jay's front office door after returning a text in the affirmative.

Here I was heading to Hegewisch, the southeast side's idea of a refugee camp for city employees. A quiet community with good stock of homes, both older wood frame and newer brick construction. For more than a century it has been more closely connected to downtown Hammond, Indiana than to Chicago, probably as Hammond remains nearer by miles. It's a favorite with newscasters in the pronunciation department, the name 'Hegewisch' has been mangled by the best in the business, mostly because none of them have ever been here.

It has a humble business district, one fast food restaurant, a community bank, several mom and pop shops of various interests, a relatively new train station on the South Shore route, a somewhat new library, the usual collection of bars, Chicago's only trailer court, and some very clannish residents who don't take kindly to 'outsiders'. A bedroom community hidden as far south and as far east as the city gets before you're tripping over a suburb. Or Indiana. Nice place to get, and stay, lost in. I never dated a girl from Hegewisch. I guess I was never quite white enough.

Steve's Lounge, a landmark of sorts in Hegewisch for over fifty years, was a favorite of off-duty cops and their kin. The place still had a walk-in telephone booth complete with folding wood-paneled door, but no phone. That was taken out during the cell phone revolution. The current owner's father, for whom the place was named, amassed a huge collection of liquor bottles and decanters of all shapes and sizes that were displayed on stacked shelves behind the classic wood bar.

The place also had a dinner and dance hall with a stage in the back, very popular when the joint was built. Now it served great fish fry dinners on Friday nights, and worked as an after funeral luncheon space. A lot of the 'new' residents liked to use it for Baptism parties.

I parked in the Lounge lot, looking around for any car that might have followed me from the East Side. Nobody. I stepped up to the corner entrance and opening the screen door, entered. Since it was Thursday night, the place only had a few people at the tables along the wall to my right, past the phone booth and the juke box, and two guys sitting at almost opposite ends of the long bar to my left. Lieutenant Vic Hanley, nursing what had to be his third drink of the night, was the second bar hugger. I made a few selections on the jukebox, getting a raised glass from the middle-aged couple nearest the nostalgic musical device, and walked over to the bar.

"You got anyone tailing me, Vic?" Patting him on the back I took a stool next to him, instinctively putting Lieu between the front door and me.

"Why the hell would I have someone tailing you for? Don't you go getting paranoid in your old age on me, Dano."

I could listen to his colloquialisms all night long. There's a dialect on the southeast side like no other in this mighty metropolis. And it comes in colors.

"Okay, Vic. Shot of bourbon, please." The waitress had seen me enter and was awaiting my order. Vic just let out a smirk again at my manners. He must have had a long day, too, passing out handbills for the mayor, or whatever it was that he had to do to keep whomever he had to answer to happy.

The waitress quickly returned with my drink. I held up my shot-glass of bourbon to meet his shot-glass of some brand of aged whiskey, a deeper brown than my drink, not taking my eyes off this old man, trying to catch a crack in that veneer of his. The old sphinx. He called for the same from the waitress, who was tending the other man at the bar.

"You got it, Sugar!" I wondered if Vic had a pet name for her, too. Maybe Toots or Trixie or Honey Bunny? I didn't know.

Everybody who was anybody in the neighborhood knew Vic, one way or another. He never came across it to me, but I wondered if he was more of a pain in the ass to those he knew the longest. I think about the wrong things when I drink.

"I suppose you have to work the wake tomorrow, huh?" I asked.

"Just to keep downtown happy is all. Aren't you covering it for the Cal?"

"A side story or two, not the main coverage." The next set-up of drinks arrived. Vic gave an uncharacteristically kind smile to the waitress. I let it pass. Maybe it was the liquor working its magic.

"With all your connections to the corpse de jour and that editor of yours assigns someone else to cover the story of the year? That must be a kick in the shins, huh, kid?" Now he was enjoying himself.

"Maybe I'm just getting too old to keep up, Vic. Ever feel that way? You know, yearning for the rocker on the porch? A condo lifestyle in South Florida?"

"This is as far south as I'm goin' 'til the good Lord plants me in Holy Cross!" Vic was kidding around, but he wasn't kidding. "What son of a bitch keeps playing those polka tunes on the jukebox?" He started looking around for a victim of his playful wrath. Then he remembered. I was the guy with all the quarters on the bar.

His shoulder sagged. "When the hell are you getting out of this goddamn neighborhood already, Dano?"

"About the time I run out of quarters, Vic." We shared a tired smile. "You wanted to tell me something?"

"Off the record?"

"Yeah, I can do that. What say we trade stories?"

"What're you gonna tell me I don't already know, Dano?"

"You better go first, Vic. My story is gonna take a while."

"Okay. Fine. About your alderman, Nicky. He is going to have to answer for his sins with the mayor, no less. This breaking away venture of his is not going to succeed."

"Was it supposed to?" Sometimes Vic forgot other people knew things, too. But again, it may have been the liquor. "I figured this was all a grandstand move on Tony's part to get other goodies from City Hall."

"Then why tie up three other alderman?"

"Greed on everybody's part. What else is new around here, Vic?" I ordered another round.

"No, not this time, my young friend. There's more to this than we will know for some time to come. Antonio will be made an example of in the City Council, and by the weekend will announce his attempt to secede from our great city was a flawed idea at best, and he will humble himself before the public and press."

I gave Vic a surprised smile. "How many drinks did you have before I got here? Have you ever met Coronado, Vic? That little son of a bitch doesn't bow to anyone outside of his mother!"

"Wanna bet?"

I thought a while. "What have you got on him, Vic?"

Without looking away from his drink, the lieutenant asked, "What story did you want to tell me, Dano?"

"Not a story so much as a confession." Vic turned and looked at me, as sober as a vicar catching the deacons having at the wine cabinet.

FRIDAY

I don't know when I'll be able forget the look on Vic Hanley's face when we parted company last night outside of Steve's Lounge. Somewhere between a father's pride and a prosecutor's closing argument. I'm sure it answered a lot of questions he'd wanted put to rest across the years with me, but to all come at once was probably too much, even for a police lieutenant. No doubt there was some disappointment there, too, along with an acknowledgement that I wasn't a kid anymore. Maybe I drank one too many. With Vic down, only Lynn to go off my short list of the people who needed a heads up from me before Saturday morning.

As usual Lynn had left early for the office, another busy day ahead for her, too, but the note she had posted to the bathroom mirror before she left was intriguing. It suggested I should interview one Maria Sosa, a new secretary in the alderman's office. Who's Maria Sosa?

No set plans 'til the afternoon left the morning open for self-improvement and deep thoughts. I worked out my usual regimen of weight training on the free weight set-up in the living room, topped off with a run around Cal Park. The lake. That beautiful shimmering, endless lake! It's why Native Americans settled here, why early settlers crossing the country stopped and made this their home. I've often wondered how suburbanites survive without seeing this view every day. To think so much of this lakefront was kept from the people for more than a century astounds me, but industry ruled back then, I guess. Take a look at the lakefront of Gary, Indiana for an example of what I'm talking about.

The last time I saw Leon Perez alive kept creeping back into the light in my skull, the day I gave him the keys to the apartment, where he would later be murdered. In my building. Bouncing around between relatives and girlfriends after getting booted out of his mom's trailer hadn't worked out for Leon, so he gave me a call. Was I supposed to say 'no'?

We met up at La Cienega on Ewing, in what used to be the neighborhood Jewel grocery store back in the '60's, converted to a Mexican grocery store in the '70's when the 'new' Jewel/Osco superstore was completed on East 106th Street. Of course that Jewel shut down in the year 2012 when the 'W' megastore opened just across the border in a place once called Robie, Indiana. Try finding that on a map today! The new owners on Ewing knew what their customers liked, providing what we'd consider exotic produce, but to their shoppers this was a little taste of Mexico. They also installed a fresh-made hot food counter in the back.

We ate lunch there, on me, as I've always had a thing for Mexican food. Leon had *carnitas y frijoles* and I had a pair of *quesadillas con queso solo y arroz y frijoles*. We also split an order of *guacamole*, which is always better freshly made, and washed it all down with a pair of refreshing *agua de horchatas*, a rice water drink. From the name and main ingredient you'd expect a starchy taste or texture in the drink, but since I first tried it years ago I've found *agua de horchatas* to be sweet, light and smooth, but not too much of any one of them.

The pair of cooks at La Cienega can whip up a great lunch in short order! Breaking bread with friends has always been a secret pleasure for me. Not being much of a cook, I've had to rely on restaurant food for any kind of complex meal, since I struck out on my own. Except when Lynn did the cooking.

Afterwards we drove over to the apartment on East 95th and I showed Leon the small, efficiency second floor layout. Since the place was already simply furnished, it was an ideal fit for my friend. As usual, he was very open about himself, sharing things I'd be hard-pressed to say out loud. He would be turning 47 years old later in the year and knew his early exploits were catching up with him health-wise.

His teeth had started falling out a few years back, but now he was experiencing cramps in his chest pectorals, describing it as if his heart was skipping beats. Leon was also having terrible night sweats, blood in his eyes and the lymph nodes in his neck swelling up from time to time.

As he put it, "I've got two good molars left that I chew with, so as long as I don't smile I'm okay. No one can tell I'm just rotting away inside."

I didn't feel sorry for the guy, and he wasn't looking for sympathy, he was too real for that crap. Leon just needed a place to crash. He said he was off drugs for good and didn't even drink anymore, but the memories were still there. When he had tried drinking some liquor recently his blood pressure went through the roof, so he knew that kind of a life was in the past.

He reasoned with himself that the can, that carburetor cleaning junk, had probably destroyed his liver and kidneys across the years of his youth when he was snorting the stuff and now had taken aim on his brain. It was about this time in the conversation that Leon asked if his younger brother, Ernesto, could crash with him from time to time. I thought it was a very good idea, Ernesto being the most stable member of his immediate family that I'd met so far.

Leon joked that he didn't even get a morning hard-on anymore, and reasoned with himself that sex wasn't everything. He had had a good sex life, nothing to complain about. He had a good laugh over that. As guys often do with other guys, he probably shared too much when he let me know that he had shaved downstairs the day before and had nicked up his *bolas* real good! Having never 'trimmed the carpet' myself, I let it go to personal hygiene choices. But I had to ask, what had that last heavy-set girlfriend of his got out of their relationship? He had another good laugh.

"You know me, Nick, that chick catered to my needs perfectly. She was just my type, submissive and cute! But her family didn't approve, so after a while out on my ass I went!" Typical for Wicho, I ask about his girlfriend's needs and he goes on about his own!

————

After a shower and shave I drove over to The Trim on East 106th Street for a haircut and floorshow. It's a six-seat barber shop with leather couch, chairs along the window side for the customers, many trophies of locally sponsored teams in the windows and a high table and chairs for the staff. There's usually some waiting time expected because of its popularity, particularly on Fridays and Saturdays. Date nights.

There are also a pair of flat screen TV's, with one endlessly airing some cable sports channel, while the other was permanently set on loud, sexy music videos. The walls had the usual items you'd expect in a barber shop: rate cards, photo examples of hair styles available for the asking, erotic artwork and personal items collected by the cutters themselves, exposing their own unique identities.

As usual, the conversations between the cutters revolved around women troubles, car troubles, gossip about each other's women and cars, and the occasional topics of local politics and community affairs. I took a seat to the right of the entrance. Manny usually cut my hair and he gave me an acknowledging nod and smile when I sat down. Rio was another cutter on this side of the shop. The third chair wasn't manned as yet.

From previous conversations I had overheard waiting my turn, I'd found out that the core of the cutters who worked here and co-owned the shop were once high school friends who had built their business up from an eight foot wide storefront space on Ewing with just two barber's chairs. They worked together, ate lunches together and often partied together after work, stag and with their girlfriends, club-hopping as you'd expect single guys in their mid to late twenties to behave.

A few of the add-ons who started cutting here since the move to the new space were older guys in their thirties, a couple of them were married and had families. The cutters were Latinos, as were most of their young clientele. All were southeast siders for most of their lives, though a few had settled in the south suburbs.

"How come you didn't make it to the club last night, Serge?" Manny asked one of the two cutters already working on customers' hair on the left side of the shop. "You missed a show, bro!"

"I wuz gonna go, man, but you know my old lady, she's getting' sick of watchin' me get drunk ev'ry time we're out!" Sergio replied, not taking his eyes off the top of his customer's head.

Rio made the sound of a cracking whip and everyone in the place had a good laugh. "Have you ever thought 'a not drinkin' so much, niggah?"

"The place was packed for a Thursday night, I couldn't believe it, you know?" Manny continued. "We got in the VIP lounge for most of the time. Only Chavo couldn't hold his liquor, man!"

"I know! Shit! I turn around and he's back in the john again!" Juan agreed. "That's probably why he's late!" Everybody had another laugh. Chavo was one of the newer cutters.

"All night long, it just goes right through him!" Manny confirmed. "He should get his kidneys checked out."

"Or his nose cleaned out!" Rio considered, getting a good-sized laugh.

"Hey, you know my lady's not like all that, man," unprompted, Sergio stuck up for his girlfriend. "She's gotta work today, she can't be out weeknights all the time."

"Did you even get lucky with that dancer that had her head in your lap, niggah?" Juan asked Manny.

"I wasn't lookin' to get lucky, niggah!" Manny replied, giving me a heads up to jump ahead of a high school boy also sitting to the right of the doorway, immersed in his iPhone. I sat down in the modern barber chair after Manny had swept up from the previous customer. He swung an oversized black coverlet over me and let it settle across my lap, tightly securing it at the back of my neck with Velcro. "The usual?"

"Yup! White guy haircut, please!" I announced, Manny giving a snicker to my usual reply.

"She puts up with a lot from me, man," Sergio continued. "Remember last year when she had that operation?" he asked no one in particular. "Man, I didn't get any for weeks!"

"You didn't get any from that, Manny?" Juan wanted to know. "I wuz sure you got some! Aww, man!"

"Hey, I get enough of what I want when I want it, don't worry about my boys, niggah!" Manny laughed it off, wetting my hair and starting to hand trim the hair on the side of my head, gathering up a row of hair between two of his fingers, cutting the longer ends of hair that extended past his fingers' width with a pair of sharp scissors. He repeated the process to his satisfaction during the conversation, and then started again on the other side of my head, with his other hand.

"Yeah, whatchu gonna get on that motorcycle of yours, niggah?" Rio asked Juan, the youngest of the cutters. That brought a smile across Juan's baby face.

"I get some, okay man? Okay! Remember that time after the concert at Excalibur's? You 'member that Puerto Rican chick? The redhead?" Juan defended his honor, making the international sign of the curves of a shapely woman with one hand while combing his customer's hair with the other.

"I remember her, man, we all thought she was a chick with a dick!" Rio got the house cutters laughing out loud. "You got some a that, niggah?"

Chavo came through the door, everybody razzing his tardiness. After making the rounds fist-bumping each member of the crew present and a few customers awaiting his arrival, he headed over to his post, the third chair on the right side of the establishment, next to Manny's chair, carrying a lunch bag along.

"You feelin' right, Chavo?" Rio asked. "You look a little off-color." Snickers from the other cutters.

"I'm fine," Chavo let him know. "Just forgot the bridge was out on Torrence." He checked his phone for messages he may have missed between his car and his chair and pulled out a charger from a counter drawer under his mirror. Manny and Rio exchanged looks of surprised disbelief.

"You forgot the bridge was out?" Rio asked incredulously. "The bridge that's been out for a year already?!"

"I can't help how long it's been out, man. I just forgot it wasn't there," Chavo explained. With a pair of scissors looming above my head I tried not to shake from the laughter inside me. Chavo took his bag of food and stepped over to the table, sitting down to eat his lunch, oblivious to everything else.

"She puts up with a lot from me, man," Sergio continued, "all the cheating, the arguments, her family. My mother! So I know she's the one, right?"

"They blew the thing up months ago, man! You forgot that?" Rio wanted to know.

"If she had a dick, man, I couldn't find it!" Juan admitted proudly, "*Y mi lengua* looked all night long!" Juan spoke out that last line with a heavy false accent, like a Mel Blanc animated character.

Chavo looked up from his food. "That's disgusting, niggah! I'm tryin' ta eat here!"

"You don't know where that Rican thing's been, niggah! Puttin' your tongue all over it!" Rio suggested.

Juan waved it off with a free hand. "How about Miller going down?" Juan asked his fellow cutters. "That got some TV coverage for the locals, man! They didn't show half his head got blown off, though!"

"What barber is gonna miss a bald man? Shit!" Rio stated more than asked. The crew had a short, uncomfortable laugh.

"His boys tried to shake us down more than once when we were still on Ewing. Fuckin' campaign contributions, they said! Fuck him!" Manny spoke up. I got kinda worried at his excitement since he was holding a straight edge razor beside my skin, trimming the line of hair around my ear with short strokes.

Rio's cell phone, sitting on the table behind him, rang with an electronic 'Rock-A-Bye-Baby' tune playing. A few of the boys started mocking the music. He checked who was calling, "One a my honeys!" and answered, holding the phone up to his ear with one shoulder, freeing up both his hands to continue cutting his customer's hair. Didn't miss a beat.

"Check out the photos online from *Baja Negra!*" Juan had searched the Internet for images from Wednesday morning, showing his customer, a high school kid, what he'd found and was saving on his phone.

"Holy shit!" the kid exclaimed, as Juan held his phone close to the boy, so he could get a good look at Joey Miller's head-wound.

"One of these days the cops are gonna pull your ass over and check out all the shit you've got on that phone, niggah, and they're gonna toss you in jail!" Rio pointed out the danger of keeping salacious materials on a personal communications device, which was news to Juan. "Don't call me for bail money, boy!"

"Its mostly porn!" Juan bragged and got back to finishing up his young customer's look, adding a dollop of mousse to the boy's hair.

"Yeah, gay porn!" Manny tossed in, giving Rio a look and a beat.

"Not that there's anything wrong with that!" Manny and Rio said in unison, with everybody else in the place having a good laugh at the old Seinfeld reference.

With his connections to the suburban mob syndicate firmly established, in his early 30's, Joey Miller ambitiously sought to expand their traditional territories for drug and vice distribution back into the south side of the city by consolidating the South Chicago gangs into one unit, which was a fete no previous criminal, nor law enforcement official for that matter, had either considered or attempted. It did not go well, for the first few years anyway, with loose cannons going off everywhere, but eventually his patience, menace and persistence paid off. He did have the unwitting help of the Chicago Police Department in 'cleaning up' the streets of the criminal element, which made it that much easier to put his own criminal element in place and on top. How many rank and file cops were injured or killed as a consequence, I don't know. What Joey didn't have for a long time, was an alderman's office in his pocket. That was going to take an as yet unknown element.

Gangs were not something new or exclusive to South Chicago, as University of Chicago studies in the 1920's listed extensive gang activities throughout the city, with emphasis on this community. Their methods would come into question years later when somebody figured out that all the researchers did was drive or walk around the neighborhood, spot a group of kids standing around on a street corner and label them a gang. Something Chicago Police Department officials would be accused of as well here and around the city, across the decades.

It took serious effort, legal and otherwise, to keep Joey's suburban connections under wraps and off the books. The old guard police knew who he really was, in the city and out, but only a few people in the press had a clue, and only a handful of them lived down here. For a lot of people, NIMBY, not in my backyard, still counts for something. So Joey could play the local hero to the Chicago organizations and powers he needed under his thumb, passing out dirty money like a drunken sailor, and still answer to his suburban syndicate masters. Having a politician or two tucked away would be a major feather. He never could get a stronghold on any previous alderman in the 10th Ward, but if he could get in with an up and coming guy, things could work in his favor. Miller didn't bother with the direct approach; he had some 'in' with the power behind the potential throne sitter. It's here I draw a blank, as to why the Coronado matriarch would risk her own son's career and the family dynasty by bringing Joey and Tony together. Is power that intoxicating?

After my entertaining haircut, I got in the Lincoln and drove to Indianapolis Boulevard taking a left, towards South Chicago. On the way I speed-dialed the 10th Ward office, making an appointment with Maria Sosa to talk, during her lunch hour, at the Service about 1 pm. Nice voice, young. I wondered what she looked like. Once on Commercial, I parked across the street from Rewer's Camera, 8944 South C.

Opened in 1957 in a former funeral parlor, which explained the canopy above the entrance, Rewer's was a staple in the community, and the only fully equipped camera shop south of Hyde Park. I remember all the Kodak paraphernalia the place had in its glass window cases when I was a kid. Mom had a camera bug, taking shots of every activity her children got involved in, from cub scouts to school plays and every family trip and holiday gathering in between. My siblings and I treasure those images now.

With the advent of phone cameras and the meltdown at Kodak, the current owner had to reinvent the place or close for good. He expanded his in-house services like film-to-video transfers, added discounts on printing and enlargement orders, and equipment rentals for weddings and baptisms. He also served a mean cup of java, turning a part of the place into a petite café, complete with new-age instrumental music playing all the time.

Sean Keaton, 36, a Black entrepreneur and local success story, another product of Bowen High giving his childhood 'hood a chance, was in the rear of his shop when I entered. A bell attached to the doorframe rang out when the door opened.

"Hey, Sean!" I called towards the back of the place.

"Hey, Nick! Want a cup a coffee?"

"You're a mind reader!"

"Comin' up!" I could see he had a customer at the magazine rack, so I sat down in the café area facing the entrance and checked my phone. I didn't have a long wait. "You still takin' it black, right?" Sean placed the oversized orange Rachel Ray coffee cup and green Rachel Ray saucer on my round table, looking like it was a Paris escapee.

"Like your men, Sean! Thanks." We shared a laugh.

"Hey, those prints you e-mailed in yesterday are ready. You want to take Polish Joe's order with you, too?" Sean stepped behind the counter.

"Yeah, I'll grab 'em both, thanks." His other customer had stepped up to the counter with a purchase. It was B. J. King. We exchanged looks. I turned back to the doorway. "You lettin' anybody in here now, huh Sean?"

"You two boys wanna wrassle you can step on outside. In my joint we keep it cool. Okayee?" Sean sensed the tension between Brent and me and had probably heard all about B. J's dip in the lake on Wednesday. From the swimmer's mouth, no doubt.

After paying for his purchase, a couple of photo magazines, B. J. took a seat at my small table, setting down his cup of coffee, a pair of new cameras dangling from around his neck on black straps. "Afternoon, Daniels."

"Brent. How's tricks?" I asked. Sean quickly joined us. How do you separate two combatants at a round table?

"You will both play nice in my shop, thank you. I don't want to have to start a wall of shame, gentlemen!" Brent and I exchanged glances.

"You're looking well, Nick." Off to a good start.

"You're looking dry, Brent." I checked my watch. Almost one.

"Now was that so hard?" Sean gave us both a fed up look and got up as another customer had entered.

"You know you're Black Beach shots of Joey Miller are getting passed around the Internet? How'd you get them back from the depths of the sea?"

"Hired some skinny white kids on their daddy's jet ski. Cost me a twenty! That's why I try to get as much up front for my captures as I can from the news syndicates. A day later they ain't worth shit, nothing anybody shoots is anymore. It's on everybody else's phone. And Christmas cards. Fucking Internet."

"New cameras?"

"Gotta be ready for anything out there! Know what I'm sayin'?"

"Have you looked into underwater housing for those things?" We both laughed out loud. Finishing the last of my coffee, I got up to leave. "I gotta go."

"We cool now?"

"Mm hmm."

"Sorry 'bout your friend. I didn't use any of his stuff, anyways."

"Thanks. Me too, Brent." I waved 'goodbye' to Sean, with the print order bags in my hand, and stepped outside.

I had to squint from the sunshine, fumbling with my sunglasses. I started to step out into traffic towards my car on the other side of the street, when that all-too familiar black Pontiac GTO zoomed past, within a couple feet of me. Damn! I could make out the back of Bernard's head in the driver's seat and Eduardo giving me a puzzled look thru the rear window. What the hell was that was about?

As their speeding car passed the intersection at 90th Street, shots rang out. I ducked down, not knowing if they were meant for me, or what! Traffic at the scene seemed to all simultaneously screech to a halt as the black muscle car continued southbound. When I stood up I could see people rushing to the sidewalk on my side of the street.

Somebody was down! I ran over, through the small crowd forming around a young Latino, probably late teens, wearing some army surplus clothing, trying to stand, but obviously wounded in a leg and an arm. Blood spattered on the cement surface, with three shiny bullet casings highlighting the area of sidewalk the crowd was avoiding. His reddish brown hair stood out in the early afternoon sun. A couple of people already had their phones out, capturing images of the scene. I hoped somebody was dialing 9-1-1. A siren sounded in the distance, but was getting closer. This kid would survive, but why was he their target? I didn't know him from anywhere. The sound of gunfire had also drawn out B. J. King and his cameras, clicking furiously at everything in sight.

Leaving my car parked where it was I sprinted the block north to the Service office. The police had already prepared the area for the expected crowds at Joey's wake at Kuzniar's funeral parlor in a couple of hours, wooden blue horses lining the sidewalk halfway up 88th Street and from what I could see, half of 87th Street, too, like on a parade day. My phone rang. It was Vic Hanley. "Hey Vic!"

"Dano! Here's a heads up! Your school chums got an APB out on their sorry selves!"

"Eduardo and Bernie?"

"Yup!"

"They just shot a kid on 90th and Commercial a minute ago! They're headed southbound right now!" I screamed in the phone.

"Shit!" I could hear Vic barking orders to his subordinates as he hung up. At that very moment three police squads zoomed past, heading to the shooting, and beyond it, after my high school chums. I didn't get the chance to ask Vic, what was the APB, all points bulletin, issued for? Before I stepped inside the office, I looked at all the people looking from their doorways and second floor windows down Commercial to the commotion. Real life still trumps everything else.

"Nick, you have a young lady waiting in the interview office," Louise let me know, nodding a look towards the glassed-in space. One of her grandsons was helping out at the office for the meeting today, hovering around Louise's desk. I was pretty sure it was Darrell, oldest son of her oldest son. Kids grow up so fast.

"Right! Thanks! Hey, Darrell!" I acknowledged, hurriedly stepping over to my desk, pulling out the laptop to check the police bulletin website.

I quickly scanned the updated site for any information... The APB was issued for the arrest of Eduardo Z and Bernard P as persons of interest in connection with the Leon Perez murder!! I sat down, looking across the room at Louise. She once again indicated the interview office with that exasperated face only she could make.

"Right!" I picked up my notepad and walked over to the glassed-in enclosure. "Hi, I'm Nick Daniels." She held out her hand, remaining seated.

"Maria. Maria Sosa." I got a small electrical charge when our hands met. "Thank you for seeing me." I closed the office door.

"Sorry to keep you waiting, there was an incident down the street a moment ago." I sat down, indicated my notepad. "Do you mind?"

"No."

"Maria, why are you here?" She was quite a lovely, not too petite Latina, light in complexion, hair almost a shade of reddish brown, with a white ribbon in it. Where have I seen her before?

"I read your blog, the one from Wednesday night. About Joey Miller."

I knew where this was going. "As a writer for the Service, Maria, I appreciate hearing from the readers, I really do. I know that some of the comments I made may have seemed pretty cold-hearted, or - "

"He was my father. At least I think so." Silence. I didn't know where this was going. I had to think.

"How can you - "

"Be sure? I'm not. My mother, our mother, has never told us who our father really was, my twin brother Angel and me."

"Then, Maria, why would you think that Joey Miller, of all people, would be your father?" She unfolded a document, a copy of a birth certificate, Puerto Rican registry, in Spanish. She handed it to me. *Joseph Miller, Ciudad de Chicago, Estados Unidos*, was listed as the father of Angel and Maria Sosa, and the U. S. as the father's country of origin.

"My mother doesn't know I have this. It belongs with her papers. I have to put it back." I handed the paper back to Maria. "Whether its true or not, I think she used it to get a job for me in the alderman's office a couple of months ago, about the time my brother started some other kind of work for Mr. Miller. Not in the office, but on the west side, Cicero, I think."

I realized I was staring at her when she began to look a little uncomfortable from my silence. She looked... familiar somehow.

"Where would your mother have met him?"

"I don't know, Mr. Daniels, she doesn't talk about it to us, but when the news came out on Wednesday morning, my mother, well, she was upset about it, like nothing before, and with Angel not coming home since - "

Holy shit! I know where I saw her before! The kid that was just shot!

"Since?"

"And then, your story came out and my mother cursed! I never heard her curse before, Mr. Daniels! It scared me! Not because of what you wrote, but she cursed him and I thought, so I found this, I seen it before but not in a long time. I knew what it was but not what it meant, you know?"

"I'm sorry if my story hurt your mother in any way, Maria. Does your brother have an army style shirt and fatigues he likes to wear?"

"No, your story was right, and good. That's what I had to tell you. I know your story is the truth. I wanted to thank you, Mr. Daniels. But how did you know about Angel wearing that silly outfit?"

"May I make a copy of your document? Not for publication, but for my own records, please?" Maria handed the birth certificate back to me. I dashed out of the inner office and made a copy, leaving it on my desk, calling Darrell over, and returning the original to Maria.

"Maria, I'm going to have Darrell drive you to the South Chicago Hospital emergency room." She quickly stood, unsure. "That incident I spoke of, down the street? I think it was your brother that was shot, but not seriously, from what I saw." She kept it together as I walked her towards the door. "He stood up and was able to walk around, so, the ambulance would have taken him to the nearest hospital - "

"I have to go there now, please!" Maria said with a genuine urgency.

Darrell's coupe was parked in front of the office and he had it in gear by the time I helped Maria into the passenger side, closing the door for her. They pulled away and took a left at 88th Street. I could see the press already setting up camera stands on the Immaculate Conception staircase, getting ready for what seemed more than likely was her father's wake. At that moment, B. J. King walked past the Service office on his way to Kuzniar's.

"Daniels! Did you get wind of what happened at Kuzniar's funeral parlor?" I shook my head. "That kid that got shot? They caught him messin' with Miller's body!"

"Who caught him doing what with Miller's body?"

"Joey's boys! Eduardo and Bernie, man! I don't know what the kid was doin' but it got them fuckin' pissed off! Hey, who was that cute chick you put in that car just now?"

"Just another satisfied customer, Brent."

"Gotta go! Catch you laters!" He walked on further north; I was about to step back inside the office, when I caught someone out of the corner of my eye, watching from across the street. He was partially hidden behind a van and turned away when he saw that I was looking back. I ducked inside, watching for a moment or two out the window, then got back to my desk, Louise following my every move from her own desk.

"It's gonna be one of them days around here! Mm Hmm!" she said, shaking her head.

———

The city big wigs started arriving early for the event, limos and caddies and a few Hummers dropping off city and county commissioners, aldermen, department heads and other elected officials, all coming together to attend a wake for who they thought was one of their own. I couldn't help but wonder how many of them came just to be sure Joey Miller was dead, rather than mourn his passing? I'd be in that line myself if I cared enough to walk into Kuzniar's, which I did not. Instead, I hung out almost directly across the street with the newsies and photographers on the steps of the Immaculate Conception BVM church, my dad's childhood parish, listening in on a few conversations, participating in a few others, and trying to dig up something on what had happened inside the funeral parlor. Brent was there, but he had grabbed a choice spot and had settled in to do his thing.

Established in 1882, Immaculate Conception BVM Church was the first Polish Roman Catholic church to open on the southeast side, the first of its kind south of the Chicago River. Completed in 1899, the church building was designed by Martin A. Carr in a monumental renaissance revival style. It's a prime example of the so-called Polish cathedral style of churches, in both its grand scale and opulence.

I've seen historic photographs at the museum of what the original altar looked like, draped in statuary on columned platforms, surrounding the central image, a larger-than-life statue of the Blessed Virgin Mary. Some older people who remember the original altar curse the day when Vatican II came to town and changed everything. Immaculate's most recent restoration, completed in 2002, included new altars designed by Franck & Lohsen of Washington, D.C. and a new plaza to the north, which gets a lot of use from its parishioners.

The on-camera reporters were lined up in the parking lane under the growing shadow of the church tower, practicing their intros, being sure to maintain enough space between themselves and rival station on-air talent so as not to overhear the others when they went 'live'. Very territorial. Most of the local networks were represented, including the Spanish language channels. I didn't know Miller was so popular in the Mexican community. All their tower trucks and vans lined both sides of 88th Street west of Commercial. What a circus!

The police kept the whole thing under control. They all knew, and were told by their commanding officers more than once, that they were under 'The Eye'. The mayor himself would be arriving within the hour to pay his official respects. I spotted a contingent of 10th Ward precinct workers and people from the office, Lynn among them.

I caught up with them after they had crossed 88th Street, walking north towards Kuzniar's.

"Lynn!" She was looking around for me, too. She stepped out of the group, waving them ahead without her. A few of the office girls chose to stay close by, waiting for their boss.

"I stopped in at your office first." We embraced. "Louise said you'd be out here somewhere. Did you meet with Maria Sosa? She never made it back to work."

"Did you know what she was going to tell me?"

"Not a clue. You're the reporter, " Lynn said with a smile and waved the last of her office girls on. We were going to be a while and we liked our privacy. "Are you going to join me?"

"Where?"

"Kuzniar's, of course," she said, a bit surprised.

"I'm not getting any closer than I am right now!" I was probably a little too defiant for my own good.

"You're not going to pay your last respects, Nick?"

"I've paid my last respects, in writing. You care to make a bet how many people are here to mourn Joey and how many are here to just be sure he's dead?"

"Does that include you, Nick?" Lynn was getting to a boiling point, quickly.

"I'm at the front of that second line, Lynn!" I wondered if I was turning red. "You don't know!"

"I didn't like him any more than you did, Nick, but this, what you're doing, is not the right thing to do!" By this time her office girls were backing away from this scene we were making, right across the street from the press hungry for anything.

"I've gotta go!" and Lynn stalked off, catching up with her girls, ignoring their questions. I just watched her go. I'm an idiot. My phone rang. It was the office.

"Do I need to remind you again that you're expected at the Service conference in five minutes?" Louise asked in that blistering voice that she could command in an instant.

"No, ma'am."

"We're looking forward to your arrival then, Mr. Daniels," and she hung up. I just stood there awhile, contemplating the mess I had made of the as yet incomplete day.

Every so often, the entire staff of the Calumet News Service would meet and talk shop. This being an extraordinary week for the southeast side and the Service, Larry Galica called everybody in to coordinate and assign coverage of everything going on or about to, leaving little to chance. Also, I figured, he was more than a little flustered at having the city press contingent literally at his doorstep, and like any proud papa, wanted us all to look and be on our best professional behavior. Besides, he got to use his Skype video conferencing paraphernalia, so he could attend the meeting without leaving the comfort and care of his bed upstairs. This technology was Darrell's specialty, and all went well, though I thought the large screen monitors showed Larry a shade redder than usual.

The conference brought many faces and ideas together, in person and in one place, and it was nice to see everybody from the Service, kind of like a family gathering, with notepads for the old-timers like me, and iPads for everybody else. I didn't get the chance to chitchat with my colleagues very often; maybe the Christmas party was the last time we were all in one room at the same time. I don't always participate in the group activities around here, but it's not like we have a softball squad.

I still had a lot of calls to return, according to my spindle. There were probably more than a few unanswered messages from my colleagues in the pile. And that invitation. I'll get to it, okay? A couple of the younger reporters, Felicia Gonzalez among them, suggested we all get together Saturday night for dinner at Roma's. Since I probably owed them all a call anyway, I figured agreeing to breaking bread together would make things even Steven.

The big show down the street from the Service office went off without a hitch. I don't think the city fathers would have allowed anything less than perfection for the cameras, or the deceased, to be remembered by. I had to wonder how many of the dignitaries prostrated themselves before the catafalque supporting the remains of their so-hailed fallen martyr? Since the press cameras were kept outside, I figured just a few, and only if they were up for reelection in a tight race. Welcome to Chicago.

The only kernel of interest I had in the interior goings on at Kuzniar's was the private meeting between his Honor, the Mayor and the Alderman of the 10th Ward of the City of Chicago, supposedly held in a back room of the establishment where the morticians kept the spare caskets and coffins for display and sale. From what I was told later on, they both entered with all smiles and back slapping, always giving good face for the public, and came out a bit disheveled, with Coronado a new shade of beige. I had to wonder, only because I'm like that sometimes, if either of them had asked the other if they wanted to try one of the crates out for size? They probably just settled their grudge match with a wrestling contest, or whipped them out to see whose was bigger. With the city's budget where it was, they should have sold tickets to the show.

Buchinski's funeral parlor in Hegewisch was a family-owned business going back decades, originally in the familiar red stone building across from the Calumet News Service office on Commercial Avenue. Its present location felt more like a home than a business, comfortable, large enough for one-at-a-time wakes, but not two. The woodwork was old world, thick and heavily varnished. I came in the side entrance, into a large foyer where several people were gathered, talking. They looked my way when I came in, but not recognizing me went back to their conversations. I weaved thru them into the main parlor, where Leon's brothers were standing beside his open casket, their mother seated in a plush high-back chair a distance back from the focal point, the deceased. A selection of floral tributes flanked the casket and candles.

"Thanks for coming, Nick." Ernesto greeted me, shaking hands, introducing me to his brothers who I hadn't seen in years.

"I'm very sorry for your loss." Words with real meaning escape us when we need them the most. How do you comfort somebody in a situation like this?

Ernesto led me over to his seated mother, staring through her tears at her dead son. "I'm very sorry for your loss." What else did I have? I took her hands in mine when she looked up at me.

"Mama, this is Nick Daniels, Wicho's friend. Do you remember him?"

"Thank you for coming, Mr. Daniels. Did you know my son well?"

"As well as anyone, Mrs. Perez." I stepped out of the way as a couple of people leaned in to greet Leon's mother. Ernesto took me aside, introducing me to his girlfriend, a very lovely Latina who didn't speak much English. Ernesto later told me that was the best kind of wife to have, not that he was thinking about getting married anytime soon.

The mood and lighting of the place was properly subdued. I left the way I came in after writing my name in the remembrance book and pocketing a couple of memorial cards, Leon's smiling face from long ago on the front, when he could smile without being self-conscious. The flip side had the dates of his birth and death, and a short prayer, ending with a plug for Buchinski's.

I stepped outside, where the heat of the day hadn't yet dissipated, passing a few young people smoking cigarettes. As I crossed the street heading to the parking lot, I thought I caught someone watching me out of a shadow. I picked up my pace and trotted the last few steps to my car, watching behind me more than in front. No one was following, but I got the hell out of there just the same. Almost home, my phone rang. It was Vic Hanley.

"Did you put your story to bed yet, Dano?"

"Hours ago."

"Ever wanted to shout 'Stop the presses!' to your editor?"

Is he kidding me? "Whatcha got, Vic?"

"The bullets pulled outta that kid this afternoon on Commercial are from the same gun that took out a tire in a bus crash twenty years ago in Missouri, Dano. Ballistics did a rush job for me. Think that's something your readers will want to know?"

"I gotta call Larry, Vic! Thanks!" I hung up the phone and pulled the car over to a stop. I jumped out of the Lincoln and started pounding on the hood, screaming. After I drained as much of the anger as I could out of my system, I woke up Larry.

"I hope I killed that little fuck!" Eduardo Z repeated like a mantra while trying to swallow a burrito whole. At least it looked that way to his waiter, from a distance. Life on the run wasn't as much fun as it looked on TV, huh boys?

"You just wounded him, bro," Bernard P said between bites. "I think I saw him get back on his feet!"

"I shoulda blown his balls off! Who the fuck he think he wuz, man? Dissing Joey's body like that! His body! Unbelievable shit-ass prick!"

"At least we got to pay our last respects, Lalo."

"One more hit and we *vamanos* this town, bro, I swear!"

Bernard's cell phone rang with the sound of an old rotary dial telephone. "'Bout time this ol' fucker calls back!" Seeing who was calling, he placed the half-eaten burrito on his plate and slid a greasy finger across the face of his smart phone, activating the device.

"Hello?" Bernard said as Eduardo leaned in to hear the conversation. "We been waitin' all day for you, man." A pause. "Yeah, I know we're hot! That's old news already! What else you got?"

"Eleven o'clock?" Bernard pulled the phone away from his head to check on its face for the time. The party on the other end continued to speak to them both. It was a man's voice, with a slight accent, European, maybe. "Yeah, we're packed! What do ya think?"

"What? Okay, where? Where? Why there?" He gave Eduardo a wise guy look, shaking his head. "Yeah, he's right here wit' me. Okay. It's gonna take us longer than ten minutes to get there, man!" Bernard took the device away from his face to disconnect. "This doesn't give us time to clean out the office 'til after, bro."

"Fuck the office!"

"Fuck the office?"

"Yeah, the cops prob'ly got it sealed, anyway, bro. Now, if we wanna be on time," Eduardo thought out loud, "if we wanna be on time? I don't like this whole set-up, bro. Ev'rybody knows our business, man, and we don't get shit outta it! And what da hell are we meeting there for? A fuckin' train yard? What are we? Stupid?? Got anyt'ing special in the car?"

"Yeah. I got a pair a Saturday nights."

"Loaded?"

"Always."

"What else you carrying?"

"A tank a gas. In case. And the b-e-l-l that Dwayne didn't want to handle, man." Bernard looked around but figured the older Mexican waiter couldn't spell in English.

Eduardo shook his head. "We're outta here! Let's get some payback on the way!" The pair left their trash on the counter along with a twenty-dollar bill and walked out of a local restaurant that prefers to remain anonymous.

When I got home from Leon's wake, Lynn still wasn't answering my calls so I gave her phone number a rest. Sometimes it's a good idea to let things cool off for a while. After looking out the window one last time, just in case, I got comfortable on the couch where bed linens and a scratchy laced pillowcase awaited me, finally hit the sack around 11:30. The day was full and done and I knocked out and drifted from paranoia into a cloud.

Two uniformed police officers sat in their squad near the viaduct entrance to Black Beach, under the Skyway Bridge. Though the evidence techs had finished their job a day earlier at the site of Joey Miller's beaching, downtown had ordered the site manned until further notice. Just up the river a long Norfolk and Southern intermodal freight train made its way across the rail lift bridge, built more than a century before. The train was headed into a yard south of Chicago's Loop, a hub for further distribution of its freight containers to other points across the country.

People of a certain gender and guys who share no interest in trains, bridges or the combination of the two may skip the next few paragraphs. Imagine ten railroad tracks crossing this point on the Calumet decades back at the height of Chicago's industrial and rail transport ages! That's why all these bridges are still standing here, though only one pair of tracks on one bridge still operates today. The two bridges just to the north of the remaining working bridge, easily recognized from their permanently raised positions, were built for the Lake Shore and Southern Railway between 1912 and 1915, from patents developed in the early 20th century by the Kansas City-based engineering firm of Waddell and Harrington. In 2006 the Chicago Landmarks Commission recommended these two, along with eight more rail bridges in the city, as designated landmarks. The towers that support the spans over the river are one hundred ninety feet tall, with each of those spans running two hundred nine feet nine inches long. They are skewed at about a fifty-degree angle.

In the space between those two and the still-working bridge once stood yet a fourth nearly identical bridge of the same double-track steel truss design, but it was dismantled by the Pennsylvania Railroad in 1965. During that demolition two workers were killed and five others injured when a steel beam being lowered onto a barge on the river came loose from its crane support.

Those first two bridges, the working and dismantled bridge, were built between 1912 and 1913 for the Pittsburgh, Fort Wayne & Chicago Railway. Currently the sole operating bridge is owned and maintained by the Norfolk & Southern Railway, with the familiar black engines wearing the galloping horse and stripes in white.

All that remains of the Straus heel-trunnion bascule bridge, the fifth rail span crossing the river here, are the fixed approach span and mechanical frame, after the *Pontokratis*, a vessel traveling inland on its first and last voyage up the Calumet, collided with the double-track bridge in 1988. Often referred to as the jackknife bridge, this structure boasted the longest bascule span in the world when it was completed for the Baltimore & Ohio Chicago Terminal Railroad in 1913. Prior to its sudden destruction, the jackknife bridge served the Chicago Short Line Railroad with some regularity. USX Corporation owned it at the time of its demise, but seldom used the bridge, so moving its freight to other trackage in the area was not difficult to do.

The loud metallic noises of the train trucks and all the clackity-clack echoes on the water and under the Skyway convinced the officers to leave their windows rolled up, so in their air-conditioned homeland security-funded SUV they didn't catch the firecracker sounds or see the flashes of light just beyond the rail bridges, on the opposite bank of the waterway.

I got the call just before midnight. It was Sergeant Bill Jankowski. He had heard the address again on his police scanner. I darted to my car, still wearing my house slippers. There wasn't time to change.

When I pulled into the alleyway just to the left of the Short Line yard tracks, my building on East 95th Street where Leon died two days before was fully engulfed in flames. Looked like the neighbor's unattached garage next door was a total loss, too. One fire company was battling the blaze, with a second crew just unpacking hoses from their rig. A water tower was already set up and pumping from Avenue N, but my place was finished. The firemen wanted to be sure this inferno didn't spread to the two buildings fronting the immediate properties.

The blaze drew a bit of a crowd for midnight, including a Short Line train crew watching from their very clean diesel switcher just north of the crossing. Police kept what little street traffic there was at this hour flowing as well as they could, herding the pedestrian by-standers to the north side of 95th Street and away from the fire crew. I had to walk away from the scene, going a few lots east along 95th.

Just what a steamy summer night in Chicago needed. All that smoke made my eyes tear up.

SATURDAY

Having gotten very used to the warm comfort of waking up in the same bed next to Lynn on weekends when she didn't have to get up for work, this morning was lonely on the couch. I knew we both had things to think over. I wondered if Lynn felt as alone as I did this summer morning. Behind our locked bedroom door. I wondered if she had read any of my blogs yet, regretting that I'd not gotten the chance to read the most important to her myself. Maybe she'd check out the Service Saturday edition on her own later. Checking my watch on the coffee table, it was barely seven. I still reeked of smoke, but there was no time for a shower as I saw I had slept through a text from Larry Galica minutes before I had woken up. I made a beeline up Ewing almost to the river, arriving in three minutes' time.

The police figured the murderer or, more likely, murderers wanted the bodies found early in the day, having left the shot and beaten remains of Eduardo Z and Bernard P draped atop the von Zirngibl burial monument in an abandoned scrap metal yard. The bullet wounds didn't finish them off, just slowed them down, judging on where they were hit, legs and arms. No easy exits to hell for these two, but rather they had been beaten to death, bones broken and chests caved in, most likely with the metal object found between their stripped naked bodies, a familiar brass bell. But no harm to their faces, not a mark, so that they could easily be identified. From the remains, the coroner's office would later conclude that the pair choked on their own blood while the murderers watched, and waited for them to die, the cold-hearted bastards.

The shootout had started between a freight yard and the rail bridges, and the police determined from the blood trails left behind that the boys had gotten some shots off themselves before they went down, wounding at least two others. Judging by the marks in the dirt, they were then dragged to their own car and driven to the scrap yard. They were beaten atop and around the square platform and raised stone, marking the gravesite of Andreas von Zirngibl, a veteran of the Battle of Waterloo, in the last remaining grave in what was a Native

American burial ground a century and a half before it was relegated to a junk heap. Samples of stains from several locations were taken by the police techs.

The police held reporters back at the gate entrance to the former scrap yard, steps away from the smoky remains of a burned out GTO, which had first attracted the police to the location. That gathered crowd included B. J. King, hugging his two new cameras close in when he spotted me, just for laughs. Engine 46 was in force, keeping the burned-out remains from reigniting.

The police couldn't stop the hovering helicopters from checking out the scene. That must have ticked off a few station managers, having to send out an expensive flying crew at a weekend rate to cover a double homicide on this God-forsaken side of town. All about the connections. Maybe they'd stick around for Joey's funeral procession, I considered, with all the city dignitaries set to show up for the press coverage. It was an election year, and they fed off each other. Some enterprising TV station had a remote controlled drone camera covering the event, making the sky show a potential air disaster-in-waiting.

Two of the reporters covering this aftermath, Arthur Josslyn of the Daily News and Justin Smith from Chicago Today, were comparing their copies of the Service Saturday print edition and recognized me, both giving me one thumb up each. I nodded in appreciation. I hadn't checked the copy out myself as yet. Seeing a familiar face on one of the officers on crowd detail, I stepped towards the blocked gate.

"Good morning, Officer Brand." I offered a handshake. He accepted.

"Hey, it's a, Mr. Daniels, right?"

"Nick. How long you been out here?"

"Couple hours, maybe a little more, since we got the call. You know, you're a topic of discussion on the police channels this morning?" I shook my head. "Yeah, some kinda article you wrote for the Service? It's getting some coverage, man!"

"Good or bad?"

"Sounds good, like something that needed saying. Gonna piss off a lotta big folks downtown! And, by the way, I'm Harold, Nick." He shook my hand again.

"Thanks, Harold."

"I'm gonna check it out myself when this shift is over. Sounds alright though, from what they're sayin' you wrote about, Miller and all his connections. This guy got himself bumped off Wednesday, was ratting out the rank and file to the gangs, man, the suits need to know that shit! That's two of his boys laid out inside right now. You need to go in?"

"No thanks, Harold, I've got it covered from out here. You might have a riot on your hands with the other press guys if you let me in!" We shared a short laugh on a grim, cloudless, hot summer morning on the southeast side of Chicago.

Police Lieutenant Vic Hanley led a small band of investigators out the yard gate and on to the driveway entrance to brief the press contingent, giving me a nod when we spotted each other. He covered the basics of the scene of the crime, short and sweet. A few questions were asked, but less were answered beyond the official briefing. I needed to get cleaned up, so afterwards I headed back home.

Lynn had left a note posted to the bathroom mirror over the sink, 'Spending the night at my Grandma's'. Great. Where's that?

I made it to Buchinski's just after 9:15 a.m. I recognized a few of the new faces in the small crowd gathered in the chapel, guys that had grown up with Leon, a few from his gang days, along with some other people I didn't know from the 'hood. The parlor had a hushed atmosphere, which is the way of funeral mornings, people speaking in whispers, families trying to keep it together, young children running around as if at a party, and everywhere that too sweet smell of decaying flowers. Wakes are different from funerals in one major way; they're not the last 'goodbye' that a funeral is. I walked around and read some of the cards on the floral arrangements. There was a nice bouquet from the Calumet News Service. Galica, had to be. There was also an expensive-looking potted live floral arrangement from Polish Jay. I didn't expect that. Kinda hit home for me, how blessed I was to have friends like that.

The funeral director stepped in front of Leon's casket, and what little volume of talk there was in the room fell silent. A priest joined him and offered prayers for the deceased, which we all recited together: an Our Father, a Hail Mary and the closing Perpetual Light, shining upon them. Somewhere a tape recording of sacred organ music played softly in the background.

The funeral director then called the pallbearers forward to pay their last respects. Having been asked the night before, I was among the six, including Leon's brothers. Wearing traditional gray gloves we said our 'goodbyes' passing by his open casket, which had among other personal effects inside, one of Leon's black homemade ninja masks. I couldn't help but smile at seeing that. We stepped off to the side as friends were then called for their last views of Leon, then his family members. Some people cried. I wondered if Leon would've just shaken it all off, calling some of his mourners a lot of fakers. I don't know. Somehow the guy never got an even break outta life.

After the graveside services at Holy Cross cemetery in Calumet City, Leon's family hosted a small luncheon in the back room of Steve's Lounge in Hegewisch. At least the food was very good, making up for the depressing atmosphere of the day. A few people who I didn't know came to the table where I sat with Ernesto and his girlfriend, wanting to shake my hand, to thank me for the remembrance to Leon I had written in the Service paper. A couple of copies of the Saturday edition were floating around the room, along with a few e-book formats of the blog, getting reactions from family and friends alike. I figured it was going to be like this all over the neighborhood. Okay. I got a look at the copy, page one, with an older portrait of me than I would have liked. Larry got it all in there!

———

Meanwhile, Joey Miller's funeral service at Immaculate Conception, from what I later heard from those present, went off like a well-rehearsed performance, until his casket was carried out of the church. At that point, in the middle of a shut-down Commercial Avenue, with all the city dignitaries present, the tower bells tolling, and the press cameras clicking and taping, the rank and file police detail turned its collective back on the proceedings when the pallbearers stepped onto the public sidewalk and off of the church steps!

Reporters could only report what they saw, not make judgment calls or editorials on the spot, except, of course, for Fox News, which later had to retract its blasting of the police leaders not being able to keep their own contingent in line. At least Fox and the other TV news outlets that covered the event live gave some credit to my article and the Service coverage for 'causing such an unprecedented public display of dissent.' I thought it took the men and women in blue a lot of guts!

───────

I really needed a break from the day and the drama and pain and people, so I drove over to Polish Jay's and spent the remainder of the afternoon cleaning a vintage Lionel O gauge Santa Fe switcher engine that was giving me some trouble on Thursday, while we both listened to 'Those Were The Days', a great old-time radio show broadcast from a western suburban college campus that aired every Saturday afternoon. It was one of my parents' favorite pastimes when they were living, kind of like comfort food for the ears. An episode of 'Fibber McGee and Mollie' or 'Our Miss Brooks' got my mind off of any problem, real or imagined, at least for the length of the show.

Jay let me have some needed time alone in his 'tree fort for grown-ups', as he often described the place, and tended to the cleaning of the deck and koi pond outside. Those fish had the life! We split a pizza for dinner on the deck overlooking the pond, at that magic hour of the day just before dusk, when the western sky lights up to rival the dawn. Of course, half way thru dinner I got a call from Vic Hanley.

"I don't suppose you caught any of the coverage from the funeral at Immaculate's on TV?" he asked.

"Not a minute, Lieu."

"Hmm. Didn't miss much. You still around the neighborhood, Dano?"

"Yeah."

"Meet me at the State Line Station gate, okay?"

"What's up?"

"I got somebody here you need to meet, Nick."

"I'll be there in 10."

"Copy that." Vic hung up. I finished one more slice of Capri's Pizza and headed for my Lincoln, leaving Jay with the clean up detail.

The State Line Station Generating Plant took three years to complete, and began operations in 1929, just before the start of the Great Depression, finally being shut down in 2012 and demolished across a few years by BTU Solutions. Designed by the architectural firm of Graham, Anderson, Probst & White in art deco style, the power plant with its towering, black smoke stacks resembled a giant exclamation point at the southern end of Calumet Park on Lake Michigan and was a landmark for generations of southeast siders. Only its magnificent arched entryway remained, at the end of Avenue G, with an E J & E and Short Line spur to one side and Lake Michigan on the other.

Operated by Commonwealth Edison under the orders of industrial magnate, Samuel Insull, and later owned and operated by Dominion Resources, it was considered a national historic mechanical engineering landmark. If the architectural firm of Graham, Anderson, Probst & White sounds familiar, think of the Wrigley Building, the Merchandise Mart, Field Museum, Shedd Aquarium and the Civic Opera House, to name but a few of their Chicago masterpieces still standing today.

Samuel Insull was, of course, instrumental in the creation and development of the Chicago, South Bend and South Shore electric railway, which today is the last of the great interurban passenger lines that once dotted America. His battles with, and payoffs to Chicago mayors, members of the City Council and other politicians and subordinates needed to complete his domination in the greater Chicago area are legendary. And complicated.

They were standing in the shadow of the archway entrance to the former power plant, waiting for me. Hanley was smoking a cigarette, talking to a man that looked like a shorter, stockier version of him.

"Nick, this is Don Steczo, a retiree of the Chicago Police Department, and a former partner of mine. He's been tailing you for a couple of days now, at the behest of your employer." Hanley and Steczo exchanged worried looks, and I got the feeling I was everybody's baby now. I warily shook the man's hand, like seeing a familiar face in a crowd in a dream. I didn't feel any calluses, as if he never had to work with his hands for a living. Then it dawned on me.

"You were at the other end of the bar at Steve's Lounge Thursday night. Yeah, I recognize you now. Thanks," I said to the man.

"Yeah, dat wuz me, kid, but dis ain't done yet." Almost a deadpan voice to match his deadpan expression.

"And Friday afternoon on Commercial across from the Service office?"

"I t'ought doze shots yesterday outta dat GTO was for you. You know when to duck!"

"Yeah, I've had a lot of practice lately." I shot a confident look at Vic. He was smoking away. "How did you beat me to Steve's that night?"

"Vic let me know you wuz goin' dare next."

"Right." I gave it a moment. "Mr. Steczo, what's not over?" He looked at Vic, and slowly walked away, checking out the State Line marker to keep busy while Vic told me the facts of life.

"Everything I have to tell you and everything you're gonna ask me is off the record, right Dano?" Vic had stamped out his cigarette and was looking directly at me.

"Sure."

"A copy of today's Service newspaper was draped over the dead heads of your high school buddies this morning in the scrap yard. That's not being released to the press, Nick."

"Okay." I wondered what the executioners were trying to prove? And how did they get an early edition of a paper that was late to press? Too many questions. "What about that kid they shot on Commercial?"

"Yeah, an Angel Sosa, if that's his real name. He was treated for his non-life threatening wounds at South Chicago Hospital and released. Your reference to the ballistics report on those bullets they removed from him was very effective in the paper. We haven't been able to find him since."

"Try Cicero, Vic. What about his sister?"

"Sister? You holding out on me, Dano?"

"I interviewed a Maria Sosa yesterday at the Service. She's a secretary in the 10th Ward office. She let me make a copy of their birth certificate. She and Angel are twins, according to the document."

"I'll need a copy of that, Dano, to confirm their ID's. What else?"

"It lists Joey Miller as their father."

"Now that is something. Tough luck for those kids, huh?"

"Yeah. From what I could find, Angel was doing something to Miller's body at Hudson's when Eduardo and Bernie walked in on him."

"Did you find out what Angel was doing?"

"No. Never did, and it was a closed casket wake. Kuzniar isn't talking, either."

Vic continued to explain the situation. "After they had expired, the unknown killers used a thick black permanent marker to write the initials 'ND' on Bernie and Eduardo's foreheads. That's not being released to the press, either, Nick. Daniels." What the fuck! I felt a ball of sweat trailing down my back like an ice cube. Vic could see that one hit home.

"Steady, Nick. You're gonna need to know this stuff. Somebody out there has a real hard on for you!"

"I get that, Vic. What the fuck?"

"We still haven't retrieved their clothing yet, that was over the top, stripping them like that. Might have been burned in their car."

"That's what's bothering you about this?"

"Easy, boy! You might want to pick up one of those Kevlar overcoats Joey was wearing the night he was bumped off."

"What good did it do him? A hoodie made out of the stuff would have been smarter, Vic."

"Yeah. I have to tell you something else about Miller." Vic handed me a manila folder. I opened it, Joey's partial face staring back at me. "The evidence techs shot this yesterday at Kuzniar's. Your initials were on his forehead, too. Looked like the same hand printed all three, to me, but the department has experts. Got any time off coming from that job of yours?"

I handed the folder back to Vic. My hand was shaking. "I'm supposed to just run away from this shit?"

"No Nick, you're supposed to survive this shit," Vic said as calmly as he could. "We think you're a target, or at least a catalyst of some kind, your articles, anyway. Getting away from this for a while would be good all around for everyone concerned. Think about it."

I just stared at him. The sun had set and the red bricks of the State Line Station gateway behind Vic glowed, the cloudless cerulean blue sky beyond shimmered in the heat at the end of the day. "Okay," I said quietly.

"Good. The sooner the better." Steczo had stepped back over to us. The conversation was at an end. We all started to walk over to our parked cars.

"See ya 'round, kid," Steczo eloquently said. I guessed he wasn't kidding.

"Hey Vic? Why did we have to meet out here?"

"Check the coverage on your phone, Dano."

I looked at the face of my phone. "Dead zone?" I asked.

"Nothing in, nothing out." Vic pointed to the sky. Satellites. "And just for laughs Nicky, the coroner's report on Joey came back. The filth was an untreated syphilitic. Had it for a decade or more. That's not being released to the press either," Vic felt obliged to share with me. "And, a, somebody cut his balls off." He gave me a sideways look as he opened his car door and got inside. "Before you get any feelings of pity for how Eduardo and Bernard ended up this morning, the latter was definitely in your apartment when Perez was strangled, from the fingerprints we retrieved, but it probably took two to hold him down, Dano." Vic gave me a nod and drove away, followed by Don Steczo.

I got in my own car and got the hell out of there. I didn't know where I was going.

━━━━━━━

Ending up back at my empty house, I figured I'd catch some TV or crack open a book or something to get my mind off the last couple of hours. I'd forgotten about the 'dinner date' with my colleagues from the Service that I'd made yesterday after the meeting. Maybe they forgot about it too, I hoped. No such luck. My phone rang. It was Felicia Gonzalez.

"Hello?"

"Nick? You still coming to dinner with us?"

"I kinda thought I'd turn in early, Felicia."

"Oh come on! You were so up for it yesterday. It's Saturday night! We don't get to spend any time together!" Her arguments were convincing, but after my conversation with Vic Hanley and Don Steczo I realized I should probably take what they said seriously. "Have you eaten yet, Nick?"

"No, I haven't made anything, yet." Like I cooked! At least I didn't lie to her.

"Well then! Why don't you meet us at Roma's?"

"My car has been giving me some trouble since it went for a swim in the lake." No lie there, either. I'm gonna get out of this alright.

"We can come get you, Nick! Mario lives on the East Side and he's driving tonight, so we can swing past your place and pick you up!" Oh good, a threesome. "We'll be there in twenty minutes. Thirty tops! Bye!" Well, she was persistent.

When I stepped into Mario's car, it became a foursome. Felicia and Mario Flores sat up front with Mario driving, while I joined Felipe Juarez, a photographer for the Service, in the back. I felt a little out of place with these three 'youngsters' but with two guys her own age range I figured Felicia would stop hitting on me, as if she ever had beyond my imagination. A little sober judgment on my part would have been a good thing. One foot in reality might have been sweet, too. Wasn't in the cards.

Under various ownership across the last couple of decades, Roma's was a great neighborhood restaurant, specializing in Italian cuisine, if the name didn't give it away. Just at the bottom of 92nd and Commercial, where it meets South Chicago Avenue, Roma's building faced both streets, with a shared parking lot behind it, where we parked. I wasn't used to getting driven around any more than I was used to sitting in the back seat. The things we do for social interaction.

The place was half-full of customers, couples mostly, when we entered, some traditional Italian music playing in the background, but we were quickly seated in a comfortable booth with menus passed around. We ordered salads, and devoured them over talk about the past week, hopes and dreams in this ever-changing field of journalism, and not too salacious office gossip. I kept being looked to for the wise old man insight. Exactly how old did I come across to these kids?

We all ordered the lasagna, which the waitress pointed out had become the most popular dish served at Roma's since being mentioned in an article for the Calumet News Service that came out earlier in the week. We stifled our laughs until her departure, like a bunch of high schoolers. If you happen to come for the lasagna, bring an appetite! The serving is extra large, and the best I've had. Looking around the table I figured everyone else already filled up on their salads, but Mario and Felipe surprised me, finishing every bit. Only Felicia had to ask for a take-out box.

Towards the end of dinner, when our mouths returned to more talking than eating, Mario and Felicia got into a 'truth or dare' contest over liquor consumption. Just what the night needed, a drinking contest between youngsters.

"Okay! Where's the nearest bar, Mario?" Felicia asked in a voice I hadn't heard from her before.

"I don't know! I'm not from around here, Felicia!"

"You work around here, don't you, Mario? Put up or shut up!" Ah, the ultimate comeback. I wondered if I was among some nondrinkers. Maybe they were inexperienced. Mario looked over to Felipe, kind of pleading for an answer to get out of it.

"Don't look at me, bro!" Felipe offered.

"96th and Commercial," I calmly interjected.

"The law firm?" Mario asked.

"Across the street," I confirmed.

Felicia burst out with "Jovial Club!" and we all gave her a look of genuine surprise. How did she suddenly know that?

We paid our bills, separate checks much to the delight of our waitress, left adequate to good tips depending on our bank account status, and drove the short length to the Jovial Club.

Brick construction after World War II around here meant boxy, faceless, utilitarian buildings, but somebody got it right with the design of the Jovial Club. Curved sides, enough flash to attract the eyes, and an interior out of some cool fifties movie made the place another little precious secret of the southeast side. Since the parking lot was full, probably some party going on in their attached hall, we parked on the street in front of the law firm and went into the Club.

The joint was on the full side, it was Saturday night after all, singles at the horseshoe-shaped bar, groups in the booths along the walls, great moody but upbeat lighting, and a Perry Como tune coming out of their choice sound system. A couple was leaving a booth on one side, which we snapped up. The young waitress was beside us in a minute.

"What'll it be, sports fans? Oh, hi, Felicia!" Okay, we were in the company of a barfly. The boys did a small double take.

"How about beers all around, guys?" Felicia was gracious enough to ask. Nods from the three of us.

"Okay, let's check those ID's, if you please," our waitress requested, and then gave me the once over. "You're cool, sir." Yeah, she's gonna get a big tip.

While waiting for our drinks, I looked around the familiar place. As we sat midway into the establishment, I could see over the bar to the glass double doors leading to the foyer separating the bar and the hall, with a direct exit to the side parking lot. I remembered from other visits here that the foyer also had the washroom entrances, so I excused myself and made my way in that direction. Felipe let the others know he had to relieve himself, too and followed. Classy guy.

That left Mario alone with Felicia, which was just fine, as I thought they had a thing for each other. Hey, why not?

Opening the glass door and stepping into the foyer, I immediately recognized a couple of faces at the hall doorway off to the right, some precinct workers for the 10th Ward organization, among them Cesar Vallez, a captain and another one of Joey Miller's neighborhood thugs. Must be where his private funeral dinner was for the locals. Damn! I tried to make it to the men's room without being noticed, but no luck, as I heard my name called out as I entered the washroom. Damn!

Felipe entered the toilet stall; you'd be surprised how shy guys can be sometimes. I used the urinal; I could care less who looked! I just knew I'd hear the door open. It did.

"Yeah, it's him! SON OF A BITCH!" Vallez screamed.

"Let it go, man!" One of his buddies, Benito Munoz, had followed Cesar inside, trying to talk him out of starting anything.

"Did you even read the bullshit this guy put out about Joey and the ward and all of us, Bennie? Didja?" He must have been drinking since the funeral earlier in the morning; he was weaving so much for a very stocky, very muscular boxing coach out of the basement of the Calumet Park field house.

I finished my business and washed up. Felipe came out of the stall, nervously, and followed my lead to the sink. I gave Cesar a calm look. "We only came in for a drink at the bar, guys." I gave what I had to say next some thought. "We'll get outta your way." I remembered Cesar from a couple of debates I had seen him attend, he always brought a crowd. A heavy hitter in the ward, he didn't have a problem reminding people what he got for them jobs-wise and what he expected in return. Cesar had been around the 10th since before Buchanan's second run in the early '90's.

"Any a my guys lose their jobs over your FUCKIN' newspaper shit, you and I are gonna settle up, Nichol-ASS!" Cute. We're back in grade school with the names.

"A little help, Benito?" I asked as I led Felipe towards the only exit besides the window outta here. Benito leaned into Cesar, making as much room for us to pass by as he could, which was just enough.

"You better head out, Nick," Benito suggested as I grabbed the door handle, stepping out into the foyer, Felipe quickly following, but I spotted three more of 'Joey's army' having a smoke outside the glass exit door to the parking lot. They stopped what they were doing to stare in our direction as we hustled ourselves back into the bar.

"Los Mios!" Felipe exclaimed as we briskly walked back to our booth, our beers awaiting.

"Check!" I called out to our waitress, who was a few booths over taking a drink order from a senior couple, smartly dressed. She gave me a quizzical look, like, 'You just got here, old man!' "We should find another place for your contest," I urged my compatriots.

"Why Nick?" Felicia wanted to know.

"It's a really great place, Nick!" Mario agreed. Felipe was already trying to pull him out of the booth.

"SHUT UP!" I explained.

Just then the dam burst. A small mob of disgruntled city employees, led by Cesar Vallez, burst thru the glass doors off the foyer, shocking the customers and staff in the otherwise sedate establishment. My first thought was to get Felicia out of harm's way as I pulled her out of the booth and aimed her towards the front door. At that moment, seconds into the siege, while the bartender screamed out the names of the city guys to no avail, a new mob was already entering the front door, blocking our departure!

"Ever piss off your readers?" I asked my stunned colleagues. "This is what it looks like!" The first punch hit home. I tried to get out of its way but only deflected it. There was screaming and I saw the bartender had a billy club in his raised hand, about to STRIKE! He must have been an ex-cop with a handy equalizer like that, I thought.

A lot of screaming and swearing and testosterone in the place. Somebody had shoved Felicia back into the booth next to ours, containing two lady patrons, still seated and enjoying their beverages. Felipe and Mario were already into it with the front door boys! I was not familiar with this side of their personalities! Maybe this was something they did every Saturday night.

I didn't have room or time to get out of the way of the second punch, right on the left side of my jaw! I could hear a bottle breaking somewhere, or was that my face? Cesar got one in, good for him, but my next right put him against the bar, and out! I didn't expect a precinct captain to have a glass jaw! Maybe that's why he only taught boxing, I don't know.

Somebody had hold of my left arm, pressing it behind me. Memo Rodriguez, another precinct worker for the ward, had had enough and was trying to peel the guy off of me, but the guy had a grip and ripped my shirt off in the process.

"Hey, Memo!"

"Hey, Nick!"

Another angry city worker rushed up behind Memo and was about to give my face his left fist, when it was caught in mid-air by a larger, older, much hairier fist! The tide was turning.

"Sorry 'bout the delay, kid!" it was Don Steczo. I could hear the owner of the enclosed fist grimace in pain, but I didn't have the time to look at his face as one last punch found my –

SUNDAY

The Alderman of the 10th Ward of the City of Chicago walked through the crowd outside Our Lady of Guadalupe Church, leading his wife, children and his mother into the sacred edifice, for Sunday Mass. Their presence usually made the services that much more special to the congregation joining them, but not so this late summer morning. While there were the usual greetings and handshakes that accompanied their weekly arrival here, something was missing. Many in the crowd had already read the Service edition from Saturday; other people in the crowd were sharing their copies with friends. Senora Serros-Coronado disapproved of this blatant disrespect and rebellion, right in front of the church, shooing away people as they offered her their copy of the Service paper! Her son, the alderman, kept a steady pace until they reached the main entrance doorway. He was on the phone, and with a nod of his head, his dutiful wife walked up the stairs with their children to the sacristy. His mother stayed at his side.

"Will you please just do this last thing for me?" he almost barked into his cell phone. He listened for an answer. "Thank you. I mean it." He hung up and, taking his mother's arm, slowly led her up the steps while the crowd walked past them. This particular church building, which opened in 1928 to serve the growing Mexican Catholic population of the southeast side, also provides the site for the National Shrine of St. Jude, Patron Saint of lost causes.

Why are the birds so damned loud?

I felt the cool of the grass on one side of my face, sunshine on the other, my hands clutching the earth to keep me from falling off. I could hear gulls caw overhead, so at least, I figured, I was close to the lake. Or were they buzzards? I just didn't want to open my eyes for some reason, my mind floated back to the long late night before, the fistfight at Jovial Club, the sounds of shattering glass or was that something else breaking? I still wasn't sure. I really need to spend more time at home. There was nothing close to pride in the memories of last night, but the grass did feel cool on my wounds. I could taste the dried blood in my mouth. Who's fist was that final punch, anyhow?

That last guy just got lucky, I guess. Steczo said I was only out for half a minute before he got us the hell outta there. Oh, yeah. Then the four of us bar buddies ended up at a little specialty joint that Felipe knew well, where the drinking contest was finally held. The joint didn't have a problem with their patrons coming in half-naked, either. The caged go-go boys added to the décor of the place. Probably out of stubbornness, I was declared the winner by the time the joint shut down and tossed us out at four in the morning. As it ended up, Felicia was the odd 'man' out as Mario and Felipe were more interested in each other than her. Or the old man!

Somebody started a lawnmower somewhere, maybe next to my brain. I must be spread out on somebody's front lawn! I slowly rolled my body onto my back, feeling muscles sore all over. I could sense a shiner coming on, but nothing felt broken. I had that going for me. Off in the distance, I could hear horse's hooves on a gravel road nearby, and they were getting louder, getting closer. I put my hands up in surrender. The horse stopped directly over me and started to lick my face!

"*TORO!*" Someone yelled. I had to protect myself from the onslaught of a drooling Great Dane.

"*PINCHA JUEVOS PERRO!*" It was the voice of my next-door neighbor, Mr. Cordero, calling to his beast from over the hedge that stood between our properties. The mutt had to have been some crossbreed between a Great Dane and a spotted zebra. It was a very big doggie that liked me too much.

"Nick! You gonna lay there all day? *PERRO!*" The animal finally finished bathing my face and trotted back to his side of the hedge, tagging the last bush as a reminder of his conquest. "*Andele jiho!* C'mon!" Cordero playfully smacked the back end of his stallion as the beast strolled passed him.

I managed a friendly wave of the hand to both of them as I struggled to get up. I also couldn't remember how I got here last night. Where my tattered shirt ended up was another mystery I didn't have an answer for. Probably the other half was working as a bar rag at the Club now. Maybe that waitress kept it for a tip. My jeans and wallet were accounted for, thank you, God.

"You better go confess your sins at Mass, Nick!" a smiling Mr. Cordero said, wagging a knowing finger in my direction. The man had three grown sons of his own, he knew. I gave him another friendly wave as I stumbled towards my front door.

"St. Kevin's has the last Mass this morning!" Cordero let me know as I fumbled with my keys and the damned front door lock, which kept moving in circles, all by itself. "Don't you be late!"

The house had been built more than three quarters of a century before for Judge Felix Buoscio, his wife, Zora, and their growing family. When the last grandchild had moved out, I fell into the chance of owning the place, which I had coveted and admired since I was a kid peddling my bike passed it on the way to Calumet Beach. There's more history here, but right now I had a growing desire to lean over the downstairs porcelain throne for a while. The comforts of home.

When I came out of the washroom I listened for any movement in the house, but I was alone. People don't break up over politics anymore, do they? I walked up the stairs, picking up my pace as well as my legs could carry me. The clock on the living room mantle chimed out at 10:22. I needed to fix that one of these days. Where was my watch?

Making time for a shower but no time for a shave, I dressed in slacks, a plain short-sleeve button-down shirt and sandals. God would have to forgive me for not wearing a tie. Hopefully there was no sin in going commando to church. Well, I was willing to risk it. Out the door.

———

On Sundays, Larry Galica watched the morning news talk shows, while being served breakfast in bed. This particular Sunday he had his pick of shows that highlighted the work of his Calumet News Service from the week just past. Mostly, in the Chicago press, the Service didn't get full credit where credit was due, and a lot of the east and west coast news outlets liked to believe that the news started and stopped with them, but Larry still took great pride from his hospital bed in the collective work of his writers and reporters. Their efforts from this past week were particularly gratifying.

Another Sunday habit is the weekly lawn care ritual. Funny how a childhood chore becomes a point of pride in the adult male animal. I guess it's because what guys really want are expensive toys with which to impress the neighbors. Lawnmowers, leaf blowers, hedge trimmers, wheel barrows, hand tools, spreaders, what's not to like, and admire, and covet?

Lieutenant Vic Hanley was a full-fledged lawnaholic and you wouldn't imagine it to look at the guy! Any given weather-permitting Sunday, there was Vic outside his bungalow with the side drive, equipment dragged out of the backyard garage, each awaiting its own turn, Vic in a white Dago T, a cigarette hanging out of his mouth.

He had grown kids and grandkids who could come over and cut his grass but this was Vic's domain, along with every one of his past-retirement age neighbors, all out on their lawns, each showing off their lawn care equipment. And their lawns. Of course in the city, the old-timers with their low-tech push mowers were the kings of grass cool. Old men in the suburbs were still into the big rig riding lawn mowers. They usually had larger lawns to go with their even more impressive equipment.

B. J. King spent most of this Sunday morning seated in front of a large screen desk computer, editing and photo-shopping images, while tunes from Quincy Jones' 'Q's Jook Joint' played on his CD player. Since he was in the upper echelon of Chicago photojournalists, what was left of them, Brent could expect an uneventful day, letting the newbie photographers cover the small weekend stories that would pop up around the town. So smoking some weed wasn't an issue; he had no reason to expect getting called up. Besides, it was a good way to practice glaucoma prevention.

On this particular Sunday, I sought some desperately needed redemption, for my pride and my less than Christian thoughts and actions from the past week.

St. Kevin's on Torrence Avenue in South Deering was one of those churches constructed at a time when the Archdiocese of

Chicago built church/school/hall combination structures, like St. Patrick's on Commercial and Sts. Peter and Paul at 91st and Exchange. This particular version of St. Kevin's had been around since 1926, though the parish, an outgrowth of St. Patrick's, was founded in 1884, to serve the Catholic population of the neighborhood that was once called 'Irondale'.

It had been a while since I attended Mass at this parish. Okay, more like years. I walked up the steps of the front entrance, blessing myself from the Holy Water dish on the side of the interior wall with my right hand as I entered the sacristy. While not a large church, the place was packed, with folding chairs on both sides of the main aisle up to the altar to supplement the crowded wooden benches.

A short Mexican man handed me a church bulletin, reacting with a step back when he looked at my war-torn face, in mock horror. Funny man. It hadn't looked that bad to me back home, but maybe it was the lighting in here, I don't know. He quickly hustled me up the main aisle, as much as I wanted to stay in the rear of the church. It's always about the getaway plan for me. The man squeezed me into an already crowded pew and rushed off to the entrance for his next victim, the people gladly moving over, away from the ugly gringo. I was only ten pews back from the altar. I knelt down to say a prayer.

Just then the band struck up. It was made up of several youths, two male violinists, the scratchy fiddling kind of course, a young lady at the keyboard with some genuine talent, and another teen-aged boy attempting the cornet, an instrument only meant to torture those suffering hangovers and music lovers everywhere. Or at least, by his interpretation. There was nowhere for the off-key sound to go but directly through my skull. I'm sure they meant to perform as well as they could, but when I walk into it I really walk into it. The congregation began to sing along with the music. At least the voices kind of dampened the cornet volume, but he seemed determined not to be outdone.

The procession entered from the rear of the sacristy, an altar boy carrying a metal cross taller than he was, followed by a pair of altar girls carrying candles with the priest celebrant, who carried the missal from which he would read passages during the service at appropriate intervals, bringing up the rear. I knew the service by heart, even with unscheduled changes to the text every other year or so via Vatican II, having witnessed and participated in thousands of Masses across my lifetime. So when I realized that this Mass would be in Spanish, I settled in for the cure, thank you, Mr. Cordero.

After the Gospel, the priest, I guessed of Mexican descent by his accent, gave the homily in Spanish, so I missed out on whatever subject he was talking about, but the people were nodding in agreement at various things he said.

Just before the 'Our Father' he invited all of the children present to join him at the altar. They all made their way at different speeds according to their skills, to the front of the sacristy, parents and families looking on with pride. It was quite a cool way to present the kids like that to the whole congregation, giving them a special place of participation in the service.

At this point in the Mass, the congregation offers each other the sign of peace, families hug, friends and strangers alike exchange handshakes and greetings. Someone in the pew behind me tapped my shoulder. I turned to look at a young man who I didn't know but somehow I did, in my mind fog. I was having one heck of a hangover.

"Mr. Nick! You came!" We shook hands, he appeared very happy to see me.

It took another moment for me to realize who I was looking at, a lot older now than the last time I saw him.

"Tommy." It was the older boy I pulled from a burning house on Houston, once upon a time. "Tommy! Hello!" Someone else tapped my shoulder from the aisle side. I turned to see a smiling Ernesto Perez with hand outstretched. I stepped out in the aisle to give him a well-deserved hug. He stepped back across the aisle to his pew, a few rows back. I turned and looked at Tommy again, remembering the invitation he had sent to the office that I had never gotten around to answering, along with all those other messages.

"It's your son's Baptism!" I said at last.

"Right after Mass. We're so glad you came, Mr. Nick! This is my family." His parents, wife and young daughter were with him. I could tell they were wondering about my face, but I shrugged it off. Tommy looked like he was going to join his mother in crying with joy. I nodded and turned, facing the altar where the priest was preparing for Holy Communion. I couldn't get the smile off my face.

There is a pause in the Mass after Holy Communion, a time of reflection, during which our young organist proved her talent with a brilliant rendition of 'Amazing Grace'. After the last blessing, completing the Mass, the priest walked down the main aisle again, waiting to greet his congregation as they left through the opened front doors. The band continued its exit music until the song had ended, many of the people remaining in their aisles, singing along until the very last notes. I sat down after letting the other people in my pew pass by. As I stretched out a bit, someone sat down suddenly beside me. It was Lynn.

"I didn't know you liked Spanish Mass - " she began, then got a look at my face. "What happened?" She held me close, eyeing my wounds, wanting to heal them with her thoughts.

"See what happens when you're not around?" I was glad to be able to hold her hand again. "Did you get a chance to look over the paper yesterday?"

"Yes, Nick. I didn't know all that, but I do now."

"I know. I guess I missed the chance to tell you in my own way and never got it back." We had a moment together, just sitting there, understanding.

Finally, Lynn looked around, "The mass is over, we should be going, Nick." I gently held her from leaving.

"We've been invited to witness a very special Baptism, babe!"

"Anybody I know?" Lynn asked. I shook my head.

"Nope!" I had that huge grin on my face again. She gave me a look that said 'I'm game for anything today!'

With Tommy's wife, parents, family and friends assembled around the baptistry in St. Kevin's, the same priest who had earlier said the Mass baptized his son. There were smiles all around and the baby boy did not make a sound during the sacrament, a perfect little guy. Lynn and I were very happy to be there, together.

Near the end of the Baptism rite, Lynn leaned close in and whispered something in my ear that I couldn't make out. "What?" I quietly asked.

"I quit," she whispered a little louder. I shook my head, not understanding the message.

"I quit the alderman's office. I quit my job, Nick." I nodded in surprised approval. We exchanged smiles. I held her close. Looking at his beautiful family, I knew Tommy was one lucky man.

A slew of microphones had been assembled outside Our Lady of Guadalupe church, each with its own logo representing a different news organization. A couple of small tape recorders were placed on the podium surface just under the large metal sign attached to the church brickwork proclaiming the Shrine of St. Jude. A crowd was assembled, mostly members of the congregation who had just stepped out of the church after Mass. More people were slowly walking by, waiting for what? They didn't know.

The Alderman of the 10th Ward of the City of Chicago stepped behind the podium, with his mother on one side of him and his wife and children on the other. A few precinct workers, who just happened to be at Mass, also made their way behind or to the side of the assembled party, along with a few city workers who owed their jobs and very livelihood to the man at the podium. The Calumet News Service had a reporter and photographer there to cover the event, Mario and Felipe not looking worse for the night before, much to the speaker's chagrin for their presence at his event. Though she was told directly not to send any notice to the Service, Lynn did the right thing for the 10th Ward of the City of Chicago.

During his brief speech, announcing a temporary halt to the proposed secession of the ward from the city, the man behind the podium was heckled by more than a few members of the crowd, a number of whom stepped away during the speech, not really giving a damn what their alderman had to say. Vic got it right, but not without sullying his own hands in the process. In the rear of the crowd, a Black photojournalist kept laughing at the speaker from behind his expensive-looking cameras, acting at times like he was high or something. The crowd gave him some room; they didn't know what to make of the guy. At the end of the speech, though they tried, the pack of reporters who did show up on short notice couldn't get the speaker to answer a single question.

———————

After saying our 'goodbyes' and 'congratulations' and holding newly baptized young Tommy Jr. for a photo opportunity, we all walked out of St. Kevin's together. I indicated my car in the side parking lot, but instead Lynn led me across the street. I didn't know where we were going; we ended up just a few houses in from the corner.

When Lynn opened an ornate metal gate, entering someone's front yard, I had to ask, "Who lives here?"

"You'll see!" We walked up the wooden steps and Lynn opened the front screen door and just walked inside. "I'm back!" she called out.

There were a lot of young kids, pre-teens mostly, gathered on an over-sized couch watching a very large screen TV on the opposite wall, some Disney animated feature I didn't recognize. I nodded to the kids, most were oblivious to anything but the movie playing, including my introduction by Lynn.

"This is Nick, everybody!" A few of them waved, politely.

"You're back! I didn't know what time to start lunch, *mija!*" A gray-haired woman called out from the kitchen two rooms over, walking into the dining room, where Lynn had led me, past an arched Spanish-style colonnade that separated the living and dining rooms.

"Grandma, this is Nick!"

"Hello! Welcome to my home! I'm so glad to finally meet with you!" She gave me a hug, then checked out my face, holding Lynn's hand. "Who did that to you, Nicky?"

"I - "

"Come in the kitchen, let's sit and talk while Lynn helps me finish lunch for the kids, I've always got a crowd here on Sundays! It's so good to meet you!" She took my arm and led me into a very modern, very stylish, very large kitchen, for such a traditional bungalow style home.

"This is a great room, Mrs. - " I started to say.

"You call me 'Grandma' too, Nicky. Everybody does, even my own kids! That's all my grandkids in the living room." She sat me down at a long island counter. "Three of my sons are carpenters, and this is what they did for their mother! It's something, huh?" It really was an amazing kitchen, complete with breakfast nook overlooking a fenced-in backyard. She hugged Lynn. "But my Erlinda was the first grandchild! I thank God for them all every day!"

"Hungry?" Lynn asked me, returning her grandmother's hug, and then slipping a plain white apron over her pantsuit.

"I haven't eaten all day."

"Nick wrote a very important article in the Calumet News Service yesterday, Grandma. Did you get the chance to read it yet?"

"It's here somewhere, I think I saw it last night on the dining room table, *mija*."

"I'll get it!" I stared bullets at Lynn as she swept into the dining room, retrieving the front section of the paper before I could beg her out of it. "Let me read the last few paragraphs to you, Grandma!" Lynn said victoriously as she scanned the front page.

"Sometimes I find it quite puzzling that people automatically choose sides where the police in this town are concerned. In our little minds they are all the real evil, or they all wear wings to work. Not a lot of gray area there for us these days, especially thanks to the power of the camera and social media. Yes, there are racists on the police force, and the corrupt and the morally straight too, just as in every line of work, from teachers to doctors, from janitors to clergymen. Maybe it's just an echo from the original sin.

"That doesn't condone the actions and inactions of individual policemen and women, but we make a fatal mistake when we lump every person in uniform with the corrupted few. The trick is to recognize our own faults in ourselves and do something about it, if it's not too late.

"In the end my friend, Leon Perez and my enemy, Joey Miller for all their flaws and achievements, met the same fate in the same community where they were born, grew up, became whatever kind of men they were destined to be. Both lived their lives as they saw fit; both were murdered in sickening ways. We, all three of us, were the product of the southeast side of Chicago, an equal opportunity stretch of neighborhoods, as long as you're not too ambitious, where the straight line and vice walk hand in hand every day. I am still alive to write these words, thank God. I'll try to recognize my own faults and work every day to be a better friend to my loved ones. That's all any of us have." Lynn set the paper down.

"That was nice, Nicky. How was Mass?" Grandma asked.

"Very beautiful, Grandma," Lynn answered, fetching a carton of eggs from the large brushed stainless steel refrigerator on one wall of the spacious room. "We stayed for a Baptism." I couldn't get over how great this room was. I think I might have been getting a little jealous, having almost given up on my own kitchen.

"Anybody we know, *mija*?" Lynn started the scrambled eggs on the island burners while Grandma pulled out a few packages of corn tortillas. All of the counters were a couple inches lower than normal, to comfortably fit the height of the lady of the house.

"Friends of Nick's, Grandma."

"Do you have family at St. Kevin's, Nicky?"

"Yes, I do, Grandma," I said, smiling at Lynn. "How about a vacation, babe?"

Lynn looked up from the skillet on the stove, kidding, "When are we leaving?"

"Tomorrow?"

AFTER

So, did Bernard P kill Leon Perez? That's everybody's guess. No fingerprints at the crime scene in the museum linked Leon to the robbery, but there were plenty of Bernie's prints in the murder apartment, indicating to the police that they knew each other for a while. In police records, Detective Ungard speculated that Leon and Bernie may have been sexually involved. I don't know.

The stone his family put over Leon's grave is quite nice, and simple. His name, year of birth and death separated by that damned dash, that short line, summing up all our lives at the end, and "Beloved Son & Friend" at the bottom. They buried him next to his cousin, the one killed years before. That was a good idea. Now neither of them would ever be alone.

The Southeast Chicago Historical Society will be looking for a new place to live and expand into, and soon. When the police returned that stolen ship's bell from the evidence files in the two scrap yard murders, it was found to be a commemorative object, not actually used on any ship. As such, when its metal content was analyzed it was revealed to be almost sixteen pounds of solid gold! Chances are that Bernard P had discovered its true nature from some Great Lakes seafaring drinking buddy. Several other missing bells and an American Shipyard company equipment manifest were uncovered in a rental unit Bernie kept in Hammond, Indiana, so he must have been looking for a while. The order of knots on the rope tied to the murder bell was the secret signal to its actual identity, like hobo marks on a fence post from a century before. Maybe Leon Perez had also found out about the bell and was silenced because of it. I don't know. Meanwhile, the Society has changed the locks and limited the number of keys issued for their space.

Thanks to the Freedom of Information Act, I was able to get some of the answers I've provided here in this wrap-up. Interviews and police logs helped in tracking down the whereabouts of key figures in the story as well. That's what a reporter does. Those revelations Vic Hanley shared with me, crime scene details and medical records, that information is still under wraps, so keep it to yourself.

The police have not released any information about the homicides of Eduardo Z and Bernard P, or if they even know anything. Reportedly a special task force has been formed between Chicago and a few western suburbs to track down possible suspects in the three unsolved murders, but that sounds too much like a line out of 'Casablanca' for me. I do know that Maria Sosa returned to Puerto Rico as she wrote me, probably to live with her mother, outside of San Juan. We've corresponded via the Internet since she skipped town, but I checked with the airline records just to be sure she was being straight with me about it. It's an unspoken rule for reporters. The whereabouts of her twin, Angel, are unknown at this time.

Lynn was another matter. While some information about the goings on in the 10th Ward office were alright for me to know after she had quit her job as executive secretary to the humbled alderman, she never did let on whatever happened to the vault cash. She gave her word to her brother-in-law and she meant it. I did get the story about Joey's bugged office by a private suburban surveillance company out of her, but not the identity of the client who ordered the bugs - yet. I love a woman who can keep secrets, even from me!

From Wednesday thru Sunday I've written about four murders on this side of town, all of people I knew, one way or another. But during that same time Chicago witnessed a total of sixteen murders, and another twenty-eight people were injured from gunfire. They will survive their physical wounds. Most of these shootings were gang or drug related, and about half of those were of innocents in the areas of the shootings. Bullets don't discriminate. Wrong time, wrong place, just wrong, but this is a part of my home town history and has been since before 'civilization' settled in for keeps, a long time ago. And we still call Fort Dearborn a massacre!

From those five days, maybe half of the shootings will be solved in a year or so and less than that number will ever be successfully prosecuted. That's something politicians never want to talk about around here, certainly not in an election year. It's fair to say that most murders in the greater Chicago area don't get solved, and the media doesn't cover most of them unless there is video footage to go along with the story. Even those that are solved tend to leave a lot of unanswered questions.

Everybody has a hand in the injustice after the fact, if not the crime itself. After all, those of us who actually bother to get up and vote keep electing the same fools who write the laws and make the deals and blame everybody else for what's wrong around here, except themselves. What do they imagine we're paying them for? If they're not doing their job, why do we keep hiring them? You try and answer any of that; Lynn and I are on holiday at an undisclosed location.

So, who did kill Joey Miller? No, not me, but thanks for the thought, God forgive me. Larry and Vic both think it was a mob hit, ordered by somebody high up who didn't like Joey's methods, or his cut of the take, or his ear studs or whatever. Last time I checked, the money found with his body had shrunk to twenty thousand in the police evidence lock-up.

With time Lynn thinks I'll get over it all, I'd like to believe that. It's just a great thing knowing she's by my side, she being such an optimist about me. Polish Jay has a phrase he likes to tout, "In this world, if you can find love, hang on with both hands." I guess I can live with that!

Officially the police don't know who killed Joey, and unofficially probably don't give a damn. I plan to find out for my own peace of mind, after all, those were my initials someone printed on Miller's forehead, and the foreheads of two other doomed souls. I do have a few leads and ideas of where to look for answers, but like Rudyard Kipling wrote at the end of 'Jungle Book', that is another story!

CPSIA information can be obtained
at www.ICGtesting.com
Printed in the USA
LVOW04*2114030916
502787LV00004B/7/P